THE SHELTER

KHALED ASHRAF

PLAIN SIGHT PRESS

Ebook ISBN: 979-8-9949421-1-6

Paperback ISBN: 979-8-9949421-0-9

First Edition, 2026

Published by Plain Sight Press

www.plainsightpress.org

Interior formatting: Ivy DeWitt, Hawthorn & Aster

www.hawthornandaster.com

Printed in the United States of America

 Formatted with Vellum

1

____

By the time Elliot found a parking spot, the street had already decided what kind of morning it was going to be.

He circled the block twice, then a third time slower, as if moving carefully could change what was already true. He knew he was late. He knew the school would note it. He also knew that rushing would make his hands shake, and the shaking would make him drop something, and dropping something would cost him minutes he did not have. That was how his mornings worked now. A chain of small failures that started before he even opened the door.

The row homes pressed close together on both sides of the street, brick against brick, each one almost identical until you looked long enough to see the differences. A cracked step that had been cracked for years. A window boarded from the inside like someone had learned the hard way that glass was not a boundary. A flag faded enough to suggest it had been there through several seasons of belief. An old wreath still hung even though the season was long gone, because taking it down required time and attention and someone to notice.

Every space was taken. Cars sat bumper to bumper, mirrors

folded in like elbows pulled tight. Someone had squeezed into a spot that barely counted, tires nudged up onto the curb, hazard lights still blinking as if that explained something. A man leaned into the trunk of a sedan, rearranging bags with the slow focus of someone trying not to go back inside yet. On the opposite corner, a woman held a toddler on her hip and stared into the street like she was waiting for an answer to arrive.

Elliot passed his own block and kept going.

He tried the next street over, then the next. He made the loop again. His phone buzzed in the cup holder. A reminder he had set for himself even though he hated reminders.

School. Pickup window. Do not be late.

He did not answer it. There was nothing to answer.

When he finally found an open space three blocks away, the only one he had seen all morning, he pulled in carefully, centering the car between the lines like precision could count as virtue. He sat there with the engine running longer than necessary. His hands rested on the steering wheel, fingers stiff, joints swollen just enough to remind him that the day would require attention. The ache was already there, low and familiar, like a warning he had learned not to argue with.

He flexed his fingers once. The knuckles resisted. His wrists felt thick, as if someone had wrapped them while he slept and forgotten to take the tape off.

He shut the engine off and listened to the quiet settlement.

The neighborhood was already awake. A delivery truck hissed as it pulled away, the sound lingering after it turned the corner. Somewhere a radio played through an open window, bass cutting in and out as someone moved around inside. A woman argued into her phone on the corner, her voice sharp with the confidence of someone who knew she was being heard. Across the street, an older man swept the same patch of sidewalk he always swept, not because it was dirty, but because it belonged to him for those ten minutes.

Everything was close. Stores. Schools. Clinics. Bus lines. Churches. Everything within reach and somehow still difficult to get to. Close was not the same as accessible. Close was not the same as safe.

Elliot opened the car door and stepped out slowly. Cold air hit his lungs and tightened his chest. He locked the car once, then again without meaning to. The beep felt louder than it should have.

He started walking back toward his row home, counting his steps without realizing he was doing it. One, two, three. It was a habit that had formed quietly. If he counted, he could measure. If he could measure, he could predict. If he could predict, maybe he could avoid the moments where his body refused him without warning.

The sidewalk was uneven, slabs shifted just enough to make him watch where he placed his feet. He could feel his knees before he could feel the ground. Some days he could ignore that. Most days he could not.

His house was narrow and tall, three stories of brick that leaned slightly forward, as if listening. The paint on the door had chipped around the handle, layers of old colors visible beneath. He paused before unlocking it, letting his shoulders drop. Letting himself be home for just a moment before the day claimed him.

Inside, the house smelled faintly of last night's dinner and laundry detergent. The staircase rose immediately, steep and narrow. The living room was quiet but not empty. A blanket lay folded on the couch the way he had left it. A toy car sat on the windowsill, its wheels still caked with dirt from the last time Marcus had played outside. The silence here was not peaceful. It was careful.

Elliot moved through the first floor quietly, the way he

always did in the mornings. His body already felt like it had been awake longer than the clock suggested. He went to the kitchen and leaned his hip against the counter while the coffee brewed. The kettle clicked off. The refrigerator hummed. The radiator made a soft sound, like it was trying to warm itself up before it could warm the room.

He rested his palms flat on the counter and let the ache spread into his wrists. He watched the coffee drip down into the pot, steady and predictable. He envied it.

He had woken before the alarm again.

It was not pain that woke him anymore. Pain came later, once the day started asking for proof. What woke him now was something subtler. A heaviness that settled into his joints overnight. A stiffness that made even the thought of movement feel like a request rather than a given. He had learned to negotiate with it. To wait. To test. To sit on the edge of the bed until his feet accepted the floor.

Some mornings, he could almost pretend he was fine if he did not move too fast.

Upstairs, Marcus slept.

That knowledge anchored him more than ever could. Not comfortable exactly. Responsibility. Weight. The kind that kept him from drifting.

Elliot poured coffee into a mug he had owned since before Marcus was born. The handle was chipped. He had meant to replace it once. He never did. He drank anyway. The bitterness was familiar, the warmth temporary.

He climbed the stairs slowly, pausing once halfway up when the tightness in his knees flared sharper than usual. He waited until it passed, breathing through it. He hated how still he had to keep moving. He hated how his body made him look like he was hesitating when really, he was deciding whether he could take the next step without falling.

Marcus's door was open just enough to let the hall light spill across the floor.

Marcus lay twisted in his sheets, one leg hanging off the bed, his arm thrown across his face. Eight years old and already sleeping like someone who had learned the day would not wait for him. His backpack sat by the dresser, half unzipped, a folder sticking out at an angle. A reminder that even childhood had deadlines.

Elliot stood there longer than necessary.

He watched Marcus breathe. The rise and fall of his chest was soft, steady. It calmed something in Elliot that nothing else could reach. He thought about waking him early, just to hear his voice, just to confirm the day was real. Instead, he let him sleep. He turned away carefully, as if sound could break the moment.

Back downstairs, the mirror by the front door caught him as he passed. He stopped without meaning to and looked at himself the way other people looked at him.

He did not look sick.

That was what complicated everything. His face held its shape. His eyes were clear. His hair sat where it should. There was nothing anyone could point to and say that is the problem. He looked like a man who should be able to show up, keep up, stay grateful.

He leaned closer to the mirror and studied the parts that betrayed him only if you knew what to look for. The slight puffiness around his knuckles. The way his shoulders sat a fraction too high like he was bracing. The dullness under his eyes that came from poor sleep and constant calculation.

"You're fine," he said quietly.

It sounded like an ending. It sounded like a dismissal. It sounded like something someone had said to him before.

He turned away and went back to the kitchen.

By the time Marcus came down the stairs, backpack

dragging behind him, Elliot had packed lunch and laid out clothes. Apple slices in a plastic container. A sandwich cut straight through the middle. No crusts. Routine mattered. It was one of the few things he could still control. Routine was proof. Routine looked like effort from the outside.

Marcus padded into the kitchen, hair flattened on one side, eyes half open.

"Morning," Elliot said.

Marcus grunted something that could have been a greeting.

Elliot helped him with his jacket, hands moving carefully so his wrists would not seize. Marcus stood still, patient in the way children became when they learned patience was required.

"You got to the gym today," Elliot said.

Marcus nodded, already drifting toward the door.

Elliot checked the time. Too close.

They walked to the bus stop together, passing neighbors who nodded without stopping. People who had lived close enough to know each other's patterns without knowing details. A man in a work uniform smoked on his stoop, eyes scanning the street. A teenage girl hustled past them, earbuds in, face set. Two little boys chased each other between parked cars while an adult voice called after them without moving.

At the corner, they waited.

"You gotta stop missing pickup," Marcus said.

His voice was casual, like he was talking about the weather. But his eyes stayed on Elliot's face. He was watching for flinches now. He was learning what questions did to adults.

"I know," Elliot said. "I'm working on it."

Marcus nodded, already accepting the limits of that answer. He had learned that some promises came with the word try attached and try did not mean the same thing as will. Trying meant the world might interrupt you and you would have to live with the interruption.

The bus came with a sigh of brakes. The door folded open.

Marcus climbed on without looking back. He had stopped looking back months ago, not out of cruelty, but because the world did not require him to. The world assumed someone would handle the rest.

Elliot watched until the bus turned the corner.

Then he stood there longer than necessary, letting the morning settle into his joints. The cold made his knees tighten. His wrists throbbed with a slow pulse. He flexed his fingers again, trying to loosen them. He could feel the day lining itself up, each demand stacked behind the next, each one requiring him to prove something before it would let him pass.

Everything was close. Everything was possible. And everything required something he did not always have to give.

He started walking back toward the car, already counting his steps again.

2

The Shelter sat behind a strip mall that had lost most of its urgency.

A nail salon with paper still taped to the windows, the edges yellowed and curling. A dollar store whose automatic doors opened late, like they were tired of pretending. A dry cleaner with hours written in marker that changed without notice. From the street, the building looked like a medical office that had stopped insisting it was temporary. Beige brick. Narrow windows. A sign bolted flat against the facade, clean and neutral, designed not to invite questions.

Elliot arrived early, which he had learned was safer than arriving on time.

Early created a margin. Early allowed for delays that did not count against you. Early suggested effort. Early suggested gratitude. Early suggested that if something went wrong later, it would not be because you had failed to try.

He parked near the back of the lot and sat with the engine running, watching people move in and out of the surrounding stores. A woman loaded groceries into the trunk of an SUV, pausing to check her phone between bags. Two men smoked near the curb, laughing about something Elliot could not hear. A delivery driver leaned against his truck and drank from a thermos, unbothered by the clock.

Elliot turned the engine off and rested his hands on his thighs. His wrists ached, the stiffness settled deep now, like it had found a place to stay. He flexed his fingers slowly. They responded reluctantly.

He stood, locked the car, and walked toward the entrance, each step measured.

The sign by the door read:

THE SHELTER

Transitional Support and Stabilization

Medical Care. Employment Readiness. Family Services.

The words were arranged carefully, each one doing a specific job. Transitional implied movement without promising direction. Support suggested care without obligation. Stabilization implied that instability belonged to the person, not the conditions surrounding them.

Elliot read it again, even though he already knew what it said.

Inside, the lobby smelled faintly of disinfectant and old coffee. The kind brewed early and forgotten. The air felt recycled. A television mounted high in the corner played a morning news program with the sound off. Captions scrolled continuously, headlines looping without context. Violence somewhere far away. Markets fluctuate. Weather warnings that did not include this block.

Men sat along the walls in molded plastic chairs bolted to the floor. Some stared at their phones, thumbs moving without urgency. Some stared at the floor; hands folded between their knees. One man slept with his head tilted back, mouth open, a manila folder resting on his chest like proof he belonged there. No one spoke.

The room had the quiet of a place where everyone was

waiting to be called, and no one expected it to mean the same thing.

Elliot approached the desk.

The woman there looked up and smiled. Her hair was braided neatly and pulled back from her face. Her badge read *Intake Specialist*. The smile was practiced but not unkind, the kind that could survive repetition.

"Name?" she asked.

"Elliot Harris."

She typed without looking at him, fingers quick and confident. The keyboard clicks filled the space between them. After a moment, she nodded, as if confirming something that had already been decided.

"We have you scheduled for intake," she said. "Most of your information is already in the system. You'll just need to confirm and sign."

She slid a clipboard across the counter.

The paperwork was thick. Medical disclosures. Employment history. Insurance information. Emergency contacts. Parenting status. A section labeled *Barriers* sat halfway down the page, bolded, with small checkboxes arranged neatly beneath it.

Elliot hesitated, pen hovering.

"What exactly counts as a barrier?" he asked.

The woman smiled again, just slightly tighter this time.

"Anything that might make consistency difficult," she said.

Consistency. The word settled heavily in his chest.

He wrote carefully, his handwriting deliberate. Chronic autoimmune condition. Unpredictable flares. Reduced hours at work. Partial custody.

The word *partial* felt heavier than the others. He paused after writing it, staring at the letters like they might change if he waited long enough. Partial meant provisional. It was subject to review. It meant there were circumstances under which someone else could decide he was not enough.

He signed at the bottom of the page. His wrist cramped halfway through his name. He finished anyway.

A case manager named Brian met him near the elevators. Early thirties. Clean polo shirt tucked neatly into pressed slacks. A name badge clipped at his waist. His voice was warm, but his eyes moved quickly, taking inventory.

"We're glad you're here," Brian said, extending a hand.

Elliot shook it carefully. Brian's grip was firm, confident. The kind of grip that assumed bodies were reliable.

"This is a good program," Brian continued. "A lot of people don't get in right away."

Elliot nodded. He did not ask how many did not. He had learned that those numbers were never useful to the person standing in front of you.

They walked through the building together. Hallways painted a soft neutral color meant to calm. The lighting was bright but indirect, like someone had worried about shadows. Posters lined the walls.

Accountability.

Progress.

Stability.

The words appeared everywhere once Elliot began to notice them, printed in the same font, the same reassuring colors. He had seen them at work. At Marcus's school. On clinic walls. They followed him like a shared language he had never agreed to learn.

"You'll have a bed, access to medical care, and employment support," Brian said as they walked. "We work closely with employers who understand flexibility."

"Flexible how?" Elliot asked.

Brian smiled, the corners of his mouth lifting just enough.

"Within reason," he said.

They stopped at a bulletin board covered in laminated schedules. Group meetings. Workshops. Required sessions. Optional sessions that did not feel optional. Times were listed in blocks that assumed availability. Mornings. Afternoons. Evenings.

"There are rules," Brian said, as if reading Elliot's thoughts. "Curfews. Check in. Expectations. Nothing unreasonable."

Nothing unreasonable on its own, Elliot thought.

"And my son?" he asked. "Visits?"

"Of course," Brian replied quickly. "We encourage family connection. It's part of stabilization. We just have guidelines."

Guidelines meant structure. Structure meant review.

No overnight stays. No unapproved schedule changes. Visits logged and time limited. Parenting is reduced to windows that could be opened or closed.

Elliot nodded. He did not argue. He had already learned which questions closed doors.

Brian stopped outside a small office and lowered his voice slightly, as if sharing something personal.

"A lot of men come in thinking this is a place to rest," he said.

Elliot waited.

"It's really a place to reset," Brian continued. "We help you get back on track."

Back to what, Elliot wondered but did not ask.

His room was on the second floor. Small but clean. A bed with a thin blanket folded tight. A desk bolted to the floor. A chair that matched the desk exactly. A window that looked out over the parking lot. During the day, the light was harsh. By evening, it would be dim. It was enough.

"It's temporary," Brian said, as if reading Elliot's thoughts. "The goal is transition."

Elliot sat on the bed after Brian left. The mattress dipped under his weight and did not recover. He rested his hands on his thighs and waited for the ache in his shoulders to settle. He listened to the building breathe. The hum of vents. The distant sound of a door closing. Footsteps that did not stop.

That night, lying awake, he stared at the ceiling and counted the cracks. He listened to the sounds of other men settling in around him. A cough that kept starting over. Someone pacing the hallway. A phone buzzing once, then stopping. Laughter, low and brief, cut off like it had gone too far.

He thought about Marcus. About school pickup times printed in bold on handouts. About the way curfews and check ins would intersect with parenting schedules that had already been negotiated carefully, each minute earned through explanation.

No one had told him he could not be a father here.

They had simply built a structure where fatherhood required constant justification.

In the morning, the building moved him along before he could resist it. Breakfast at a set time. Intake appointments stacked back-to-back. Names called from a list. Forms signed. Instructions given in calm voices that did not invite questions.

By afternoon, Elliot understood something without quite naming it.

The Shelter was not a place of punishment. It did not need to be.

It was a place where compliance felt like relief.

3

———————

Marcus's school sat wedged between a laundromat and a church that had been boarded up long enough for the sign to fade completely.

The building itself was older than most of the families who passed through it now, brick darkened by years of weather and waiting. The front steps dipped slightly in the middle, worn down by thousands of small feet moving in and out every day. A banner stretched across the entrance, secured with zip ties that had been replaced more than once.

WE BELIEVE IN EVERY CHILD.

Elliot read it every time he came.

Parking was worse here than at home. He circled the block twice, then slowed on the third pass, scanning for anything that could be defended as a space. Cars lined both sides of the street, some too close to the curb, some not close enough. A minivan idled with hazard lights on while a woman hurried across the street with a child pulling against her hand. Someone double parked near the corner, engine running, door open like a promise they could not keep.

Elliot eased into a spot that barely qualified, the back of his car jutting into the street. He shut the engine off and sat there, hands resting on the steering wheel. The ache had moved again, settling deep in his shoulders, a dull pressure that made him aware of each breath. He waited until it softened enough to stand.

Inside, the hallway smelled like floor cleaner and paper. The scent was sharp, meant to suggest order. Children's voices echoed from somewhere deeper in the building, rising and falling in uneven waves. Sneakers squeaked. Lockers slammed. A bell rang, too loud for the size of the space.

Elliot signed in at the front desk. The pen was chained to the clipboard. He wrote his name carefully, aware of how deliberate his movements had become. He printed his phone number slowly, double-checking the digits. Mistakes had a way of staying on file.

Ms. Delgado met him near the office, her expression open but purposeful.

"Thanks for coming in," she said, already turning down the hall.

He followed her past classroom doors with windows cut into them, each one offering a brief glimpse of controlled chaos. Bulletin boards lined the walls. Perfect attendance charts. College pennants. Rules written in friendly fonts.

Just outside the main office, a large bulletin board caught his eye.

Laminated letters in bright colors spelled out a phrase he had seen in dozens of schools over the years.

I AM SOMEBODY.

Smaller signs were taped beneath it, some handwritten, some printed.

My voice matters.

I am important.

My future counts.

The board was neat, well maintained. Someone had taken time with it. The edges were straight. The tape was fresh.

Elliot slowed without meaning to.

He had taught in buildings like this once. Had stood in front of rooms where children recited those words every morning, voices uneven but earnest. He believed they mattered. He still did. What he wondered now was how long the words lasted once they left the wall.

The meeting room was small, just big enough for a table and three chairs. Student artwork covered the walls. Crayon houses. Misspelled slogans. A sun with too many rays. Marcus's drawing hung slightly crooked near the door. A house with three windows and a stick figure standing just outside it. The figure's hand hovered near the door but did not touch it.

Ms. Delgado took a seat across from him and opened a folder.

"We just want to check in," she said. "Nothing serious."

The counselor joined them a moment later, closing the door gently behind her. She introduced herself and sat, folding her hands on the table.

They talked about attendance first. About focus. About patterns. The language was careful, practiced. Concern without curiosity.

"He's a bright kid," the counselor said. "We just want to make sure he's supported."

Elliot nodded. He had learned this rhythm. The way reassurance often preceded record keeping.

"I do pickup when I can," he said. "Sometimes I get held up."

"We understand," Ms. Delgado replied, already writing something down.

They talked about consistency. About routines. About the importance of predictability. Words floated close to judgment without ever touching it. Everything was framed as guidance. Everything sounded reasonable.

"At this age, stability is everything," the counselor said. "Kids need to know who will be there."

The sentence settled between them. Not accusation. Not concerned exactly. Something closer to documentation.

Elliot shifted in his chair. His wrists ached where they rested against the table edge.

"I'm present," he said. "I communicate."

"And we appreciate that," Ms. Delgado said, smiling. "We just need to ensure we're aligned."

Aligned meant legible. Aligned meant predictable.

The counselor slid a paper toward him. A copy of the school's dismissal policy, highlighted in yellow.

"We're required to follow protocols," she said. "Repeated waiting raises concerns."

"What kind of concerns?" Elliot asked.

She hesitated, just long enough to matter.

"Safety," she said finally. "Appropriate supervision."

Elliot nodded. He did not argue. He had learned that arguments became notes.

At the end of the meeting, Ms. Delgado closed the folder.

"We'll continue to monitor and reach out if concerns come up," she said.

Monitor. Reach out. The words sounded gentle. They did not feel that way.

Outside, Elliot's phone buzzed before he reached the sidewalk.

Missed call.

Shelter Case Management.

He imagined the note already being entered. Missed contact. Follow up required. He stood there for a moment, phone in his hand, watching parents' stream past him. Keys already out. Voices raised toward children halfway down the block. No one appeared to be counting minutes the way he was.

He has not called back yet. He needed to breathe first.

On his way out, he passed the bulletin board again.

Someone had added a new line at the bottom in pencil. The handwriting was uneven, the pressure light, as if the writer had not wanted to be seen.

I am somebody when I do what I'm supposed to.

The words were faint, almost erased.

Elliot stopped. He read it twice. He looked around, but no one was watching. He considered finding someone to tell. He considered taking a picture. He considered all the ways that noticing something could turn into a responsibility he could not carry.

He turned and kept walking.

Outside, the cold air tightened around him. He started toward the car, his shoulders stiff, his knees already protesting. His phone buzzed again.

This time, he answered.

"Mr.. Harris?" a voice said, bright and professional. "This is Brian from The Shelter. Just checking in."

"I'm at my son's school," Elliot said.

There was a pause, brief but intentional.

"Of course," Brian said. "We just need to make sure we're staying on schedule."

"I'll call you back," Elliot said.

"Please do," Brian replied. "It's important."

Elliot ended the call and leaned against his car, closing his eyes for a moment. He felt the weight of the building behind him. The weight of the phone in his hand. The weight of a sentence written in pencil by someone small enough to believe it.

He started the engine and pulled back into traffic, already late for something else.

4
____

The ambulance was still there when Elliot stepped out of his row home.

It sat crooked in the narrow street, half blocking traffic, red lights bouncing off brick facades and windows that had seen too much already. A police cruiser idled behind it, engine running, patient. Neighbors stood on stoops in coats and slippers, arms folded, watching with the practiced stillness of people who had learned not to react too quickly. They watched without moving, not because they did not care, but because caring did not change what happened next.

Three houses down, paramedics moved with the calm of routine. Not rushing. Not hesitating. A young man sat on the curb with his head in his hands. A woman stood behind him, one palm pressed into his shoulder, the other gripping a phone like it had stopped offering answers. A backpack lay open near the curb, its contents spilling onto the pavement. A notebook. A hoodie. A half-crushed water bottle rolling slowly when the wind touched it.

Elliot did not stop to ask what had happened. He had

learned the language of these scenes. Whatever it was, it had arrived quietly and would leave paperwork behind.

He locked his door and moved down the steps carefully, his knees already stiff. Cold air cut into his chest, sharp enough to remind him that his body did not distinguish between his emergencies and anyone else's. His wrists were swollen again, thick at the joints. He rotated them slowly, testing, then let his hands hang at his side.

The street offered access to everything. A clinic on the corner. A pharmacy half a block away. A grocery store that stayed open late. A bus line that ran so often you could hear it before you saw it. Social services offices tucked into buildings with clean signage and long waits.

Everything was close. Everything required more than proximity.

Parking was three blocks away again. Elliot slid into the seat and sat for a moment before turning the key. His fingers felt heavy. Reluctant. He flexed them once, then again, until they obeyed.

He drove to work with the heater on too high because the cold made the stiffness worse. At red lights, he rolled his shoulders, trying to loosen them without drawing attention. He watched other drivers sip coffee, talk into phones, adjust mirrors, move through the ordinary choreography of morning without negotiating with their joints.

At work, he arrived ten minutes early, which he had learned was safer than arriving on time.

Early suggested effort. Early suggested gratitude. Early gave people less to write down.

The security guard nodded at him as he passed.

"You good?" the guard asked.

Elliot nodded back. It was the kind of exchange that let a person pass without explanation. The guard did not ask twice. Elliot did not offer more.

The office was quiet in a way that made his shoulders tighten. Not focused. Not calm. A quiet that suggested a decision had been made and was waiting to be delivered properly.

He reached his cubicle and sat slowly, easing his body into the chair as if the chair might punish him for moving too fast. His knees pulsed. His wrists throbbed. He opened his computer and watched his inbox refresh.

A message from HR sat at the top.

Mandatory meeting. Today. 1:30 p.m. Conference Room B.

Below it was a note from Denise.

Please come to my office when you arrive.

Elliot stared at the screen until the words stopped shifting. He clicked nothing. He moved nothing. He could feel the day rearranging itself around that meeting.

He reached into his bag for his notebook and felt an envelope he did not remember putting there.

No stamp. No return address. Just his name printed neatly.

His stomach tightened before he opened it. He knew what paper like this usually meant.

Inside there was a notice from the city about unpaid tickets. Final warning. The amount was not devastating. It was worse. It was just enough to start something he could not afford to finish. Just enough to trigger late fees, holds, collections, complications. Just enough to become an emergency without being treated like one.

He folded it and put it back in the envelope, then set it on the desk as if it might stay quiet if he did.

A few minutes later, Denise appeared at the edge of his cubicle holding a folder.

"Can you step into my office for a second?" she asked.

Her voice was calm. Always calm. Calm was how you delivered consequences without calling them consequences.

Elliot stood slowly, feeling his knees resist before giving in. He followed her down the hallway past posters about care and culture, the kind companies put up to remind people they had values. One read **WE TAKE CARE OF OUR PEOPLE** in large letters. Another said **COMMUNICATION IS KEY** above a photo of smiling coworkers whose job was to smile.

Denise closed the door behind them and remained standing. Elliot stayed standing too. Sitting felt like agreement.

"I want to check in," she said. "How are you feeling lately?"

Elliot knew the question was not about care. It was about record keeping.

"I'm managing," he said.

Denise opened the folder.

"We've noticed some inconsistencies," she said. "Attendance. Timing. Missed windows."

Elliot's jaw tightened.

"I communicate," he said. "I'll let you know when I have appointments."

"We appreciate that," Denise replied, marking something on the page. "And we want to support you."

Support. The word landed like a warning.

She slid a document across the desk.

Performance Improvement Plan.

The language was clean. Measured. Written as if bodies were predictable and time belonged to the company. Expectations were listed in bullet points, each one reasonable on their own. Timely arrival. Reliable coverage. Consistent communication. Notice of absences. Documentation of medical appointments.

Documentation. The word appeared three times, each time framed as policy.

"This is standard," Denise said. "It's a way to support you."

Elliot read the first paragraph twice. His eyes snagged on the same sentence.

Failure to meet expectations may result in further corrective action, up to and including termination.

The sentence did not threaten. It was recorded.

"What happens if I can't see it?" he asked.

Denise's expression did not change.

"The goal is improvement," she said.

Elliot looked at the signature line. His wrist ached as he picked up the pen. He signed anyway. He felt his hand cramp halfway through his name, the letters turning slightly uneven. He kept going until it was finished.

Denise took the paper back and placed it neatly in the folder, as if the document were a complete task rather than a decision about his livelihood.

"We'll meet weekly to review progress," she said. "And I really do believe this will help."

Help, Elliot thought, did not usually come with a countdown.

Back at his desk, the office felt louder without sound. He could sense attention he did not want. People typed. Phones rang softly. Conversations started and stopped when he passed. He opened a spreadsheet and stared at it without seeing the numbers.

He ate half his lunch and pushed the rest away. The sandwich tasted like paper.

At one o'clock, his phone buzzed.

School pickup reminder.

A minute later, another message appeared.

Shelter check in today. Please confirm.

Elliot stared at the screen until his eyes blurred slightly. His calendar lives in three places now. Work. School. Shelter. Each one assumed it was the only one that mattered.

At 1:15, the HR reminder popped up again.

Mandatory meeting. Conference Room B. 1:30 p.m.

Elliot stood, then stopped. He checked the time. He calculated distances. He calculated the consequences.

His phone rang.

"Mr. Harris?" a woman's voice said. Bright. Professional.

"This is Mrs. Landon from Marcus's school. I'm calling to follow up."

Elliot leaned against the wall between cubicles, where the carpet met the hallway.

"Yes," he said.

"We are required to ensure a consistent dismissal plan," she said. "Repeated waiting raises concerns."

The same language. The same calm. The same framing.

"What kind of concerns?" Elliot asked, even though he already knew.

"There are protocols," she replied. "We want to support your family."

Support. Again. Always before the restriction.

Elliot looked down the hallway toward Conference Room B. The door was still closed. People moved past it without looking.

"I'll be there today," he said.

"Thank you," Mrs. Landon replied, relief entering her voice as if compliance had solved something.

He ended the call and stood still, phone in his hand. The air around him felt thinner. He could feel his pulse on his wrists.

His screen flickered with a new email notification.

From Shelter Case Management.

Reminder: Missed check-ins may impact eligibility. Please confirm attendance today.

The language was careful. No threat. No accusation. Just the suggestion that losing your bed would be a consequence of your choices rather than the structure you were trapped inside.

Elliot returned to his desk and sat, slowly. His knees trembled as he lowered himself into the chair. He placed both hands flat on the desktop and stared at them for a moment. Thick fingers. Puffy knuckles. Hands that looked normal if you did not watch them struggle to open.

He opened his calendar again. Then again, as if looking harder would create time.

At 1:28, he walked toward Conference Room B.

The meeting itself was brief. There were a few people he barely knew. An HR representative with a calm smile. A manager reviewing new procedures as if procedures were protection. Elliot listened and nodded when nodding was required. He did not speak. Speaking created records.

At 2:12, his phone buzzed again.

School dismissal begins at 2:50.

At 2:15, another message.

Shelter check in closes at 3:00.

At 2:20, Denise walked past him in the hallway.

"You, okay?" she asked, the same tone as the security guard, but with a pen behind it.

"I'm fine," Elliot said automatically.

Denise smiled and kept walking.

Elliot stood there for a moment after she left, feeling the day narrow around him. Not dramatically. Not all at once. The way a hallway narrows when you're not paying attention until you realize your shoulders almost touch the walls.

He thought about Marcus standing on the sidewalk after school, backpack on, scanning the street. He thought about the Shelter receptionist checking a list, noting who had not arrived. He thought about Denise's folder, neat and ready, waiting for the next weekly review.

He could feel proof being demanded from every direction.

He walked back to his desk, grabbed his coat, and moved toward the exit. His knees burned with each step. His wrists pulsed. His heart felt too loud in his chest.

Outside, the cold air hit him again. He started walking faster than he should have.

Halfway to the parking lot, he stopped to catch his breath. He looked at the office building behind him. Clean windows. Bright lobby. Posters about care.

He looked down at his phone.

A new email from HR had arrived while he was in the meeting.

Subject: Follow Up Documentation

He did not open it.

He started walking again, already late, already being written down.

5

Kiana's block looked like Elliot's from a distance.

Same row homes. Same narrow streets. Same fight for parking. But once he stepped out of the car, the differences announced themselves quietly. The sidewalk here was even poured all at once instead of patched over time. The streetlights worked. Trash day actually meant something. Lids stayed on cans. Bags did not split open and bleed onto the curb.

People nodded when they passed each other, not because they were friendly, but because they were used to being seen.

Elliot parked half a block away and walked slower than he wanted to. His knees protested with each step, the stiffness deep now, settled. He did not rush. Rushing always cost him later and later was already crowded.

Kiana opened the door before he knocked.

She stood there with her coat on, keys already in her hand, her body angled toward departure even as she stepped aside to let him in. Her hair was pulled back. Her face held the kind of alertness that came from managing too many schedules at once.

"They called again," she said.

No greetings. No accusation. Just information.

"I know," Elliot said. "They called me too."

The living room was clean in the way that came from effort, not ease. Not decorative. Maintained. Marcus's backpack rested by the couch, unzipped, one strap twisted. A math worksheet peeked out, corners bent from being folded too many times. On the coffee table sat the school binder, thicker than it needed to be, stuffed with notices and handouts that all said important in different fonts.

Kiana moved through the room with purpose, setting her keys down, picking them back up, then finally leaving them on the counter like a decision she had made and did not want to revisit.

"They said it's becoming a pattern," she said. "They said it like it was something he was doing."

Elliot sat carefully, lowering himself onto the couch. His wrists ached now, a dull pulse that followed his heartbeat. He rested his hands on his thighs and waited for the room to stop tilting slightly.

"I went to the meeting," he said. "They didn't say much different."

Kiana stopped moving and looked at him.

"Did you explain what's going on with you?" she asked.

Elliot exhaled slowly.

"What explanation would help?" he asked. "That I'm sick but I look fine. That my schedule belongs to three different systems. That I'm trying to keep a job that's documenting me while I prove I deserve a bed at a place called The Shelter."

Kiana's face softened, but she did not interrupt. She leaned against the counter, armscrossed loosely, listening.

"They don't hear that," Elliot continued. "They hear excuses."

She nodded once.

"I'm not trying to push you out," she said. "I'm trying to keep them from making decisions without us."

"Without me," Elliot said quietly.

Kiana did not argue.

Marcus came out of his room then, backpack still on, shoes half untied. He stopped when he saw Elliot, his face unreadable for a second longer than it should have been. Eight years old and already learning how to pause.

"Dad," Marcus said.

Elliot stood, pain flashing through his knees, and forced his body to move like nothing was wrong. Marcus crossed the room and pressed into him, arms tight around his waist. The sudden weight stole Elliot's breath. His balance wavered for a second before he found it.

He closed his eyes and held on.

"Are you staying?" Marcus asked, his voice muffled against Elliot's jacket.

"For a little," Elliot said.

Marcus pulled back and studied his face, the way children did when they were checking for truth. His eyes moved carefully, taking inventory.

"You gonna pick me up tomorrow?" he asked.

The question landed hard.

"I'm gonna try," Elliot said.

Marcus nodded. Trying was something he understood. Trying meant the world might interrupt you and you would have to live with the interruption.

At the table later, Marcus pushed peas around his plate, lining them up along the edge. Kiana moved between the stove and the sink, wiping down surfaces that were already clean.

"They make us line up," Marcus said suddenly.

Elliot looked up. "Who?"

"At school," Marcus said. "If your ride isn't there, you gotta stand by the wall."

Kiana paused at the sink.

"They say it's so everyone's safe," Marcus continued. "But everybody can see you."

Elliot felt something tightening in his chest.

"What do you do while you wait?" he asked.

Marcus shrugged. "I just wait."

"Do you worry?" Kiana asked gently.

Marcus considered the question.

"Not really," he said. "I just know you'll come when you can."

Elliot smiled, thin.

"I got rules," he said, trying to keep his voice light.

Marcus looked up.

"Like school?" he asked.

Kiana turned from the sink.

"Yes," Elliot said. "Like school."

Marcus nodded slowly, filing it away like information that would matter later. He went back to arranging peas.

After dinner, Elliot helped Marcus with homework. He leaned over the table, his wrists stiff, his shoulders tight. Marcus read aloud while Elliot corrected gently, careful not to rush him.

"You don't gotta stay if you're tired," Marcus said at one point.

Elliot froze.

"I'm okay," he said.

Marcus nodded again, satisfied, as if he had done his part.

When Elliot stood to leave, Kiana walked him to the door. The hallway light buzzed softly overhead.

"They watch dads differently," she said, not unkindly. "You know that."

Elliot nodded.

"I know," he said.

"They assume mothers adjust," Kiana continued. "They assume dads explain."

Elliot rested his hand on the doorframe, steadying himself.

"I don't want them deciding things because they think you're unreliable," she said. "I need you to understand that."

"I do," Elliot replied. "I just don't know how to be more reliable than I already am."

Kiana looked at him for a long moment, then reached out and straightened his collar, a small familiar gesture that felt heavier than it should have.

"Just keep showing up," she said.

Outside, the air felt heavier. Elliot walked back to his car slowly, the image of Marcus standing by a wall sitting in his chest like a warning. He sat behind the wheel for a moment before turning the key, hands resting on the steering wheel.

Showing up, he thought, was not the same as being counted.

He pulled away from the curb, already rehearsing explanations he hoped he would not need.

6

The shelter changed at night.

Not dramatically. Not in ways anyone could name. The lights dimmed slightly. Voices lowered. Movement slowed. The building settled into a version of itself that felt more honest, like it no longer had to perform care once the day staff left.

Elliot lay on his bed with his hands folded over his chest. The thin blanket barely held heat. The mattress dipped beneath him and stayed there, as if it had learned his shape quickly and decided not to let go. In his pocket, the letter from the school was folded small, creased so many times it felt soft at the edges. He had read it once. He did not need to read it again.

Around him, the sounds of other men filtered through the walls. A cough that kept starting over, like the body could not decide how much air it needed. Someone pacing the hallway, footsteps measured, counting without counting. A phone buzzing once, then stopping. Somewhere down the hall, a laugh rose briefly and cut off, like it had crossed a line.

Compliance had its own rhythm here. Quiet. Predictable. Exhausting.

In the morning, his body did not cooperate.

His wrists felt locked, fingers thick and slow, like they belonged to someone else. His knees resisted standing, swollen with heaviness that made the floor feel farther away than it should have been. He sat on the edge of the bed and waited, counting breaths the way he had learned to do when his body demanded negotiation instead of movement.

When he finally stood, the room tilted slightly. He waited again. He had learned patience the hard way.

Downstairs, breakfast moved efficiently. Trays slid along the counter. Names were called. Instructions given. Elliot ate without tasting it, aware of the clock on the wall. Everything here ran on time blocks that did not bend.

At the clinic wing, the receptionist asked his name without looking up.

"Elliot Harris."

She slid a form toward him.

"Any changes?" she asked.

"Yes," Elliot said.

She nodded and pointed to the waiting chairs.

The nurse practitioner was kind in the way people were when they believed kindness was enough. She asked him to rate his pain. She asked about sleep. She asked about stress. Her pen moved steadily across the page.

"Stress worsens symptoms," she said.

"I need something that helps," Elliot said. "I need to function."

She paused and looked at him, really looking, as if noticing him required intention.

"We manage symptoms," she said. "Acceptance is part of treatment."

Acceptance sounded like permission to stop asking.

By midmorning, his joints had loosened just enough to move without stopping every few steps. He sat across from Brian in the same tidy office as before. The desk was clear except for a laptop and a framed certificate that faced outward.

"I need flexibility today," Elliot said. "Pickup is at three."

Brian nodded slowly, folding his hands.

"You have an employment readiness workshop at three," he said. "Attendance is required."

"I wasn't told about it," Elliot replied.

"It's on your schedule," Brian said, turning the laptop slightly as if to prove it.

Elliot leaned forward.

"I'm a father," he said.

Brian's smile tightened, almost imperceptibly.

"And we respect that," he said. "Family connection is important. We just need you to understand how these things are reviewed."

"What happens if I leave?" Elliot asked.

Brian paused, choosing his words carefully.

"It becomes a compliance issue," he said. "We would have to review your status."

Review. The word settled heavily between them.

"And if I stay?" Elliot asked.

Brian's expression softened, as if relieved.

"Then you're demonstrating commitment," he said.

Commitment to what, Elliot wondered but did not ask.

He left the office with his chest tight. Outside, the air felt thick, undecided. The sky hung low, gray, without rain. At the bus stop, people stood in silence, each one carrying their own calculations.

The bus was late.

Elliot checked the time. Two thirty.

His wrists throbbed. His knees burned. The letter in his pocket felt heavier with each passing minute, as if the paper itself were counting.

Across the street, a group of kids in uniform walked past, laughing, backpacks bouncing against their shoulders. They moved freely, unbothered by schedules that had not yet learned their names.

Elliot imagined Marcus standing by the wall again, backpack on, eyes scanning the street. He imagined Kiana checking her phone. He imagined Brian checking a list.

The bus did not come.

He checked the time again. Two forty.

Every system he was part of demanded proof. Proof of effort. Proof of worth. Proof of gratitude. Proof that he understood the rules even when the rules contradicted each other.

He stepped off the curb and started walking.

Each step sent a flare of pain through his knees. His wrists burned with every swing of his armsHe did not stop. He counted blocks instead of minutes. One. Two. Three. He focused on the ground ahead of him, the cracks in the sidewalk, the uneven slabs.

Halfway down the street, his phone buzzed.

Shelter Check In: Please confirm attendance.

He kept walking.

Another buzz.

Reminder: Missed activities may impact eligibility.

He slid the phone into his pocket without looking.

By the time he reached the next intersection, his breath became short and shallow. His legs trembled. He leaned briefly against a lamppost, steadying himself. People passed without looking. No one stopped him. No one recorded the effort.

He pushed off and kept going.

He did not know if he would make it on time. He did not know what would be written down. He did not know which choice would cost him more.

He only knew that somewhere, a child was waiting by a wall, and that waiting had already started to feel normal.

He crossed the street and kept walking.

7

———

By the time Elliot reached the school, his knees felt like they belonged to someone older.

He had underestimated the distance the way he always did when he was trying not to admit what the day was asking. The streets blurred into each other. Blocks that should have been familiar felt longer, like the city was stretching itself out to test him. His breath came shallow. His wrists burned from the swing of his arms, each movement a reminder that his body kept receipts.

He slowed near the corner and forced himself to straighten. If he arrived looking like he had been running, the school would see panic instead of effort. He had learned that effort did not count if it did not look calm.

The front of the building was crowded with parents and older siblings and strangers in work uniforms stopping on their way home. Cars pulled up and rolled forward in slow waves. Horns sounded briefly and then stopped, not anger, just impatience.

Elliot checked the time.

Three twelve.

He stepped onto the sidewalk and felt the tightness in his chest sharpen. The banner above the entrance moved slightly in the wind.

WE BELIEVE IN EVERY CHILD.

He walked faster, then immediately paid for it. A flare shot through his right knee, sharp enough to make his vision flicker. He gripped the railing, waited, then kept going.

Inside, the hallway smelled the same as it had earlier. Floor cleaner. Paper. A faint sweetness from cafeteria food that had already been served. The building was quieter now, emptied by the day's noise. This was in between times. The time for waiting.

He reached the front desk and leaned slightly forward, trying to keep his breathing even.

"I'm here for Marcus Harris," he said.

The woman behind the desk looked up. Her eyes did a quick scan of his face, then dropped it on her computer.

"Name?" she asked, as if he had not just said it.

"Elliot Harris."

She typed. Her expression did not change.

"One moment," she said.

Elliot waited.

Behind him, two mothers stood with coats still on, phones in hand, talking softly about weekend plans. Their voices carried without effort. Their bodies did not appear to be negotiating anything.

The woman at the desk stood and disappeared through a door marked STAFF ONLY. Elliot listened to the latch click behind her and felt something in his stomach sink.

When she returned, she was not alone.

Mrs. Landon stepped out with her posture straight, a smile already prepared. The smile did not reach her eyes.

"Mr. Harris," Mrs. Landon said.

Elliot nodded. "I'm here."

"We were concerned," she said, the word shaped carefully. "Marcus has been waiting."

"I'm sorry," Elliot said. "The bus didn't come. I had to walk."

Mrs. Landon tilted her head slightly, as if evaluating whether his explanation fit the approved categories.

"We understand there are delays," she said. "But we need a consistent plan."

"Where is he?" Elliot asked.

"He's in the main office," she replied. "With Ms. Delgado."

Elliot followed her down the short hallway. His knees felt unstable again, but he kept his pace steady. His hands hung at his sides, fingers swollen, trying not to curl.

The main office door was open. Marcus sat in a plastic chair near the wall, backpack on his lap. His feet did not touch the floor. He swung them slowly, not playing, just moving because stillness was hard. He looked up when Elliot entered, and his face changed quickly, relief moving across it before he tried to hide it.

Elliot felt his throat tighten.

"Hey," Elliot said softly.

Marcus stood and walked toward him, careful, like he was not sure how close he was allowed to be in this space. Elliot bent slightly and hugged him. Marcus's arms wrapped around his waist, tight and familiar.

"You, okay?" Elliot asked.

Marcus nodded into his jacket.

Behind Marcus, Ms. Delgado sat at a desk with a folder open. She looked up and smiled, politely.

"Hi, Mr. Harris," she said.

Elliot released Marcus and straightened slowly.

"I apologize," he said. "It took longer than I thought."

Ms. Delgado nodded as if apology was a check box.

"We just need to talk briefly," she said. "About dismissal."

Elliot looked at Marcus. Marcus's eyes stayed on the floor now.

Mrs. Landon remained near the door, armscrossed loosely, as if her presence was incidental.

Ms. Delgado's voice stayed calm. "As we discussed, repeated waiting raises concerns. We have procedures."

Elliot swallowed. "I'm doing my best."

"We appreciate that," she replied. "But the plan cannot depend on your best. It has to be reliable."

Reliable. The word landed in his chest like a weight.

"What are you asking for?" Elliot said.

Ms. Delgado folded her hands. "We're asking for an alternate pickup plan. Someone listed who can be called if you are delayed."

Elliot stared at her. "His mother handles most days."

"She is not always available," Ms. Delgado said. "We need redundancy."

Redundancy sounded like a technical term, like Marcus was a process that required backup systems.

"I don't have family nearby," Elliot said.

Mrs. Landon shifted slightly, still silent.

Ms. Delgado nodded slowly. "Do you have a neighbor? A friend? A coworker?"

Elliot felt heat rise in his face. He thought about the Shelter. The rules about visitors. The guidelines. The way every connection became something to log.

"I'll figure it out," he said.

Ms. Delgado wrote something down. The pen scratch on paper sounded loud in the small office.

"Also," she said, not looking up, "Marcus mentioned you have been staying somewhere else."

Elliot froze.

Marcus's shoulders tightened.

Elliot kept his voice even. "We are in a temporary situation."

Ms. Delgado looked up, her expression careful again.

"Thank you for sharing that," she said. "We want to support your family. There are resources."

Resources. The word again. The same softness. The same doorway that narrowed as you approached.

"We're fine," Elliot said.

"We still need documentation," Ms. Delgado replied. "Just to ensure we have appropriate information on file. Housing stability impacts student support plans."

Housing stability.

Elliot nodded, because nodding was safer than arguing.

Ms. Delgado closed the folder.

"Marcus can go," she said, as if permission was hers to grant.

Elliot reached for Marcus's backpack. Marcus held it tighter.

"I got it," Marcus said quietly.

Elliot let him.

They walked out together. Mrs. Landon opened the door wider, smiling again.

"Thank you for coming," she said.

Elliot did not answer. He held Marcus's hand as they stepped into the cold.

Outside, Marcus walked close, shoulder almost brushing Elliot's arm. Elliot could feel him monitoring his pace.

In the parking lot, Marcus looked up.

"Did you get in trouble?" he asked.

Elliot blinked. "No."

Marcus waited.

Elliot corrected himself. "Not exactly."

Marcus nodded slowly, as if filing it away.

They walked toward the bus stop. Elliot's knee flared again halfway there, sharp enough to make him slow. Marcus slowed with him without being told.

"You hurting?" Marcus asked.

"A little," Elliot said.

Marcus looked ahead. "You should sit more," he said, like it was simple.

Elliot almost laughed. The sound would have come out wrong, so he held it back.

At the corner, Elliot checked his phone.

Three missed calls.

Shelter Case Management.

A new message blinked on the screen.

Please return the call immediately. Review required.

Review.

He could feel the day tightening again, pulling him back toward another office, another folder, another calm voice.

He called.

After one ring, Brian answered. His voice was warm, as if nothing had happened.

"Mr. Harris," he said. "We were trying to reach you."

"I was at my son's school," Elliot replied.

"Of course," Brian said, pausing briefly. "The reason for the call is that you were marked absent from the workshop."

"I told you I had a pickup."

"It was still scheduled," Brian said. "And you also missed check in."

"I was walking," Elliot said before he could stop himself.

Brian exhaled softly, a sound that could be sympathy if you wanted it to be.

"Okay," Brian said. "Here's what we need. You have to come in tonight for a compliance review. It's a brief meeting."

Elliot's stomach dropped.

"What time?" he asked.

"Six thirty," Brian replied. "Please be on time. This is important."

Elliot looked down at Marcus, standing beside him, hand still in Elliot's.

"I can't," Elliot said. "I have my son."

There was another pause, slightly longer.

"We respect that," Brian said. "But you also have program requirements."

"I'm trying to do both," Elliot said.

"That's what we're helping with," Brian replied. "But we need your cooperation."

Cooperation. Another word that sounded like care if you did not listen closely.

"What happens if I don't come?" Elliot asked.

Brian's voice stayed calm.

"Then we have to document noncompliance," he said. "And that may affect eligibility."

Eligibility.

Elliot felt his throat tighten. He looked at Marcus again. Marcus was watching him now, eyes steady, not asking, just listening.

"I'll figure it out," Elliot said.

"Thank you," Brian replied, relief in his tone as if agreement solved something. "We'll see you tonight."

Elliot ended the call and stood there, phone in his hand.

Marcus waited a moment, then asked quietly, "Is it the Shelter?"

Elliot stared at him.

"How do you know that?" Elliot asked.

Marcus shrugged. "You always look like that when they call."

Elliot's chest tightened again, not pain, something else.

"Yeah," he said. "It's the Shelter."

Marcus looked down at the sidewalk.

"Are you gonna get kicked out?" he asked.

Elliot swallowed hard.

"No," he said, too fast. Then he tried again. "I don't know. I just gotta go talk to them."

Marcus nodded slowly, like he already understood that talk meant proof.

They rode the bus back toward Kiana's neighborhood because it was closer, because it was safer, because Kiana's block still held shape when Elliot's life did not. Marcus sat by the window, watching buildings pass. Elliot sat with his hands folded, keeping his wrists still because movement made the ache louder.

At Kiana's door, Elliot hesitated before knocking. He could already imagine her face, alert, tired, managing.

She opened the door with the same coat on, the same keys in her hand, as if she had been waiting for a call that never stopped.

"You got him," she said.

"I got him," Elliot replied.

Kiana's eyes moved over Elliot's face, reading.

"What happened?" she asked.

Elliot stepped inside and lowered his voice.

"They want a compliance review," he said. "Tonight."

Kiana's mouth tightened.

"Because you picked him up," she said.

"They won't say it like that," Elliot replied. "But yeah."

Kiana looked toward Marcus, who had gone to the couch and pulled his backpack onto his lap. He opened it and took out a worksheet without looking up.

"They called me earlier," Kiana said quietly. "The school."

Elliot's stomach dropped again. "What did they say?"

Kiana leaned against the counter, armscrossed.

"They asked if everything was stable," she said. "They asked if we had a consistent plan. They used the word stable like it was a favor."

Elliot closed his eyes for a moment.

"They want documentation," he said.

Kiana stared at him. "Of what?"

"Where I'm staying," Elliot replied. "Housing stability."

Kiana exhaled, slow.

"They're building a file," she said.

Elliot opened his eyes.

"Yeah," he said. "They are."

Marcus looked up from the couch.

"Am I in trouble?" he asked.

The question was quiet. Not dramatic. Just direct.

Elliot walked to him and crouched carefully, ignoring the flare in his knees. He placed a hand on Marcus's shoulder. Marcus's body was small and solid under his palm.

"No," Elliot said. "You didn't do anything wrong."

Marcus studied him. "Then why do they keep talking like that?"

Elliot did not answer right away. The truth was too big for the room.

Kiana stepped closer, her voice gentle.

"They just have rules," she said to Marcus. "School has rules."

Marcus nodded, but his eyes stayed on Elliot.

Elliot felt something in him settle, heavy and clear.

"Hey," Elliot said to Marcus. "You did good today."

Marcus's face softened slightly.

"I was waiting by the wall," Marcus said. "But I didn't cry."

Elliot's throat tightened again.

"I'm proud of you," Elliot said.

Marcus nodded, accepting praise like it was information.

Elliot stood slowly, using the arm of the couch for support. His wrists pulsed. His phone buzzed again in his pocket.

A reminder.

Compliance Review. 6:30.

Kiana watched him.

"Are you going?" she asked.

Elliot looked at Marcus, then back at Kiana.

"I have to," he said.

"And if you don't?" Kiana asked.

Elliot swallowed. "Then I lose the bed."

Kiana's face did not change, but her eyes sharpened.

"And if you go," she said, "what happens to him tonight?"

Elliot stared at the floor.

The house was quiet. Marcus turned back to his worksheet, pencil moving carefully, as if staying busy could keep the world from shifting.

Elliot felt the pressure from both directions.

School. Shelter. Work. Family.

Each one demands the same thing in a different voice.

Proof.

He looked up at Kiana.

"I'll go," he said. "I'll come back."

He did not know if it was a promise or a prayer.

8

The compliance review took place in a room that looked like it could have belonged anywhere.

Neutral walls. A table with four chairs. A laminated sign taped near the door reminding everyone to silence their phones. The clock on the wall ticked loudly, marking time that did not belong to anyone in the room.

Elliot arrived early.

Early was safer.

He signed in at the front desk and took a seat in the hallway, hands folded, wrists aching. The building hummed around him. A television played quietly somewhere down the hall. A copier whirred and stopped. Voices rose briefly, then lowered. Nothing sounded urgent.

At six thirty-two, Brian stepped out and smiled.

"Mr. Harris," he said. "Thanks for coming."

The smile suggested this was a good thing.

Brian led him into the room. Two other people were already seated. A woman Elliot did not recognize with a tablet resting on her lap. A man with a legal pad and a pen held precisely between his fingers. Everyone nodded politely.

"Have a seat," Brian said.

Elliot sat. The chair was hard. His knees protested as he lowered himself. He kept his hands still on the table because movement drew attention.

"This won't take long," Brian said. "We just want to review today."

Review again.

Brian spoke first. He listed facts. Missed workshop. Missed check in. No advance notice. The words were neutral, stripped of context. Elliot listened, nodding when nodding was required.

"I was walking to pick up my son," Elliot said when there was a pause.

Brian nodded sympathetically. "We understand that parenting responsibilities come up."

The woman with the tablet looked up briefly, then back down.

"But the workshop was scheduled," Brian continued. "And check in is a core requirement."

"I told you I had a pickup," Elliot said.

"Yes," Brian replied. "And that's noted."

Noted. The word landed flat.

The man with the legal pad spoke next. His voice was calm, practiced.

"Part of stabilization is demonstrating reliability across commitments," he said. "When conflicts arise, we look at how choices are made."

"I chose my son," Elliot said.

There was a brief silence.

"No one is saying that was wrong," Brian said quickly. "We're just looking at patterns."

Patterns again. Always patterns.

The woman with the tablet cleared her throat.

"We also need to address housing disclosure," she said. "We

received an inquiry from an external institution requesting verification."

Elliot's stomach dropped.

"What institution?" he asked.

"The school," Brian said. "They contacted us to confirm your address for record consistency."

Record consistency. The words felt clinical. Clean.

"I didn't authorize that," Elliot said.

Brian folded his hands. "We're allowed to verify participation when child welfare or safety is involved."

"It wasn't," Elliot said. His voice came out tighter than he meant.

The man with the legal pad looked up. "The inquiry was framed as support," he said. "No action was requested."

No action. Just confirmation.

Brian leaned forward slightly.

"Here's where we are," he said. "You missed the required components today. That places you out of compliance."

Elliot waited.

"Normally," Brian continued, "this would trigger a warning."

Normally.

"But because of the external inquiry," the woman added, "and the documentation already on file, we have to escalate."

Escalate. The word sounded heavier than it looked.

"What does that mean?" Elliot asked.

Brian glanced at the others, then back at Elliot.

"It means we need to pause your placement," he said.

Pause. Not removal. Not discharged. Pause.

"For how long?" Elliot asked.

"Seventy-two hours," Brian replied. "It's a standard reset period."

Reset again.

"Where do I go?" Elliot asked.

Brian hesitated just long enough to be honest.

"We can provide a list of alternative shelters," he said. "If space is available."

Elliot felt the room tilt slightly.

"I have my son," he said. "I picked him up. I will take him to school."

Brian nodded, sympathetic again.

"We understand this is disruptive," he said. "But we also have to maintain program integrity."

Integrity. Another word that asked him to accept the decision as moral.

"Is this permanent?" Elliot asked.

"No," Brian said quickly. "Of course not. This is corrective, not punitive."

Corrective. Like his body. Like his parenting. Like his life.

The woman slid a piece of paper across the table.

"Please sign to acknowledge," she said.

Elliot looked at it. The language was familiar now. Temporary suspension. Noncompliance. Review pending. Signature line at the bottom.

His wrist cramped as he picked up the pen. He signed anyway.

When he stood, his knees almost buckled. He steadied himself against the table, then let go.

Brian stood as well.

"We'll contact you," he said. "Stay reachable."

Reachable meant exposed.

Outside, the night air was cold and sharp. Elliot stood on the sidewalk for a moment, unsure which direction to go. The building behind him looked unchanged. Lights on. Doors opening and closing. Another name would be called tomorrow.

He checked his phone.

Two missed calls from Kiana.

A text followed.

What happened?

Elliot typed, erased, typed again.

They paused my bed.

He stared at the screen, then added:

I'm coming.

He started walking.

The streets were quieter now. Stores closed. Windows dark. A bus passed without stopping. Elliot walked block after block, counting to keep himself up right. His knees burned. His wrists throbbed. His breath came short, but he did not stop.

When he reached Kiana's block, the lights were still on in her living room. He stood at the door for a moment, hand hovering near the bell.

Inside, Marcus was doing homework at the table. He looked up when Elliot entered.

"You came back," Marcus said.

Elliot nodded.

"I said I would," he replied.

Kiana stood by the counter, arms crossed. She read his face immediately.

"They paused you," she said.

"Yes," Elliot said.

"For choosing him," she said.

"They won't say it like that," Elliot replied.

Kiana exhaled slowly.

"Where are you staying?" she asked.

Elliot looked around the room. The couch. The floor. The space that already held more than it should.

"I don't know yet," he said.

Marcus watched them, pencil frozen in his hand.

"Are you gonna sleep here?" he asked.

Elliot hesitated.

Kiana answered before he could.

"For tonight," she said.

Marcus nodded, satisfied.

Elliot sat heavily in a chair. His body finally gave up trying to hold itself together. He rested his hands on his knees and stared at the table.

Outside, a car passed. Somewhere, a siren sounded briefly and then faded.

Nothing dramatic happened.

No one yelled.

No one threatened.

No one broke a rule.

A bed was simply no longer available.

Later, when Marcus was asleep, Elliot lay awake on the couch, staring at the ceiling. The house made small settling noises. Kiana moved quietly in the kitchen, cleaning something that did not need cleaning.

Elliot thought about the words that had followed him everywhere.

Support.

Stability.

Compliance.

Eligibility.

He understood now that none of them were promises.

They were conditions.

And once you saw that, you could not unsee it.

9

____

Morning arrived without asking where Elliot had slept.

Light crept through the blinds at Kiana's place and settled into the room like it belonged there. The house woke up gradually. Pipes clicked. The refrigerator hummed. Somewhere outside, a car door slammed and an engine turned over. Ordinary sounds, unbothered by the shift that had already taken place.

Elliot woke stiff and disoriented, his body slow to register the unfamiliar angle of the couch, the borrowed blanket pulled too tight across his chest. His knees ached sharply when he tried to stand. His wrists felt thick, uncooperative. He sat for a moment and waited, counting breaths, letting the room come back into focus.

From the kitchen, he could hear Kiana moving quietly. Cabinets opening. A mug set down carefully. The sound of coffee pouring.

Marcus padded down the hallway in sock feet, backpack already on his shoulders.

"You up?" Marcus asked, stopping when he saw Elliot.

"Yeah," Elliot said. "I'm up."

Marcus nodded, satisfied, and went into the kitchen.

Elliot pushed himself to his feet and followed, moving slower than he wanted to. He leaned briefly against the doorway while his knees steadied.

Kiana stood at the counter; phone pressed between her shoulder and ear.

"Yes," she was saying. "This morning. Thank you."

She ended the call and looked at Elliot.

"That was the school," she said. "They wanted to confirm who's picking him up today."

Elliot nodded.

"They asked if you were still staying at the shelter," she added.

"And?" Elliot asked.

Kiana poured coffee into a travel mug and snapped the lid on.

"I said no," she said. "I said it's temporary."

Temporary again. The word stretched to cover more ground than it should have.

Marcus sat at the table eating cereal, spoon clinking softly against the bowl.

"Can you walk me today?" Marcus asked.

Elliot hesitated.

"My knees might slow me down," he said.

"That's okay," Marcus replied. "We can be late."

Elliot felt something tightening in his chest.

"No," he said. "We won't be late."

They left together, the three of them moving through the morning like a unit that had been reconfigured without instructions. Outside, the air was cold and bright. Elliot felt the stiffness deepen with each step, but he kept his pace steady.

At the corner, Kiana stopped.

"I'll handle pickup," she said. "I switched shifts."

Elliot nodded.

"I'll call the shelter today," he said. "Figure out next steps."

Kiana studied his face.

"Don't let them keep saying temporary without dates," she said. "Temporary has a way of sticking."

Elliot nodded again.

Marcus hugged him quickly before crossing the street. Elliot watched him go, backpack bouncing lightly against his shoulders, and felt the familiar weight settle back into his joints.

After they left, Elliot walked in the opposite direction, slower now, conserving energy. He stopped at a bench halfway down the block and sat, letting his knees rest. He checked his phone.

Three emails from the Shelter.

Subject: Placement Status Update

Subject: Required Follow Up

Subject: Next Steps

He opened the first.

Your placement remains under review. Please remain reachable. Failure to respond may impact eligibility.

Remain reachable.

He closed the email without replying.

He called the number listed instead.

After two rings, a voicemail answered.

"Please leave your name and availability," the recording said.

Elliot hung up without leaving a message. Availability was not something he could promise.

He sat on the bench and watched people pass. A man in a suit talking loudly into his phone. A woman pushing a stroller, moving with practiced ease. A delivery truck blocking half the street, no one honking because everyone understood it would move eventually.

Everything continued.

By noon, his joints were screaming. He walked to a pharmacy and bought a cheap heating pad, paying with a card that made him flinch when the receipt was printed. He sat in the back corner of the store, the pad plugged into an outlet meant for phone chargers and waited for his body to loosen enough to stand again.

His phone buzzed.

Shelter Case Management: *Please confirm receipt of messages.*

He typed back.

Received.

A response came almost immediately.

We need to schedule a follow-up appointment.

When? Elliot typed.

A pause.

We'll let you know.

He slipped the phone back into his pocket.

In the afternoon, he tried to work remotely, sitting at Kiana's table with his laptop open, but the numbers blurred. His wrists cramped when he typed. His focus drifted. He closed the computer and stared at the wall instead.

By three o'clock, he was exhausted in a way sleep could not fix.

Marcus came home animated, talking about a class project, about a kid who got sent to the office, about how long they had to wait after the bell rang. Elliot listened, nodding, asking questions when he could.

"They make us stand by the wall again," Marcus said casually. "But Ms. Delgado says it's just until everyone's ride comes."

Elliot nodded, though something inside him sank.

At dinner, Kiana checked her email while Marcus ate.

"They sent me a form," she said, not looking up. "The school. Just asking about living arrangements."

Elliot set his fork down.

"What did you say?" he asked.

"I haven't replied yet," Kiana said. "I wanted to talk to you."

Elliot leaned back in his chair. His knees throbbed. His wrists felt hot.

"Say it's temporary," he said.

"That's what I plan to say," she replied. "But they'll ask again."

Elliot knew she was right.

Later, after Marcus was asleep, Elliot sat alone on the couch. The house was quiet except for the hum of the refrigerator and the faint buzz of the heating pad against his knees.

He opened his phone and scrolled through messages he had not answered. HR. Shelter. A reminder from the city about the tickets.

Everything was still open. Nothing resolved. Every door partially ajar, just enough to keep him from resting.

He thought about the word *review*. How often it appeared. How it never seemed to end.

The system did not need him to fail.

It just needed him to remain in motion.

Trying.

Explaining.

Waiting.

Outside, a bus passed, brakes hissing softly, then pulling away. Elliot watched its reflection slide across the window and disappear.

Tomorrow would arrive the same way morning always did.

Without asking where he had slept.

10

———

Elliot learned quickly that displacement could look like routine if you repeated it long enough.

By the third morning on Kiana's couch, his body had started to anticipate the angle of the cushions. His knees protested less when he stood, not because they hurt less, but because he had stopped expecting ease. The ache settled into him like the weather. Present. Familiar. Not negotiable.

He woke before the alarm, as he always did now, and lay still for a moment, listening.

The house was quiet. Kiana's footsteps in the kitchen. The low sound of a faucet running. A cabinet closing gently. Marcus turned in his room, sheets rustling. The refrigerator hummed like it was keeping time.

Elliot sat up slowly and waited for the room to steady. He rubbed his wrists with his thumbs, pressing into the thick joints until sensation returned. He stood and walked toward the bathroom, careful not to make noise.

When he looked in the mirror, he saw the same man he always saw. Face intact. Eyes clear. Hair in place.

He did not look like someone who was losing ground.

That was the part that made everything harder to explain.

In the kitchen, Kiana handed him a mug without asking.

"School emailed again," she said.

Elliot nodded as if he had expected it, because he had.

"What did they say?" he asked.

Kiana opened her phone and read from the screen.

"They want an updated emergency contact list," she said. "They want a consistent dismissal plan. They want verification of address."

Verification. Again.

Elliot stared at the coffee, watching the surface tremble slightly from his hand. He tightened his grip until it steadied.

"I can put you down," Kiana said. "If you want."

Elliot looked up.

"As an emergency contact," she clarified. "Not for anything else."

Elliot nodded, then paused.

"That makes it real," he said.

Kiana's expression tightened.

"It is real," she replied.

Elliot did not argue. His throat felt too tight for that.

Marcus came in wearing his backpack, shoes half tied. He sat at the table and started eating without being told.

"Do I have to go early again?" Marcus asked, mouth full.

Elliot blinked. "What do you mean?"

Marcus shrugged.

"Ms. Delgado said if my ride is late, I should go to the office," he said. "So, I can wait there instead."

The office. The wall. The waiting relocated, made official.

Elliot looked at Kiana. Kiana looked back at him.

"That's fine," Kiana said to Marcus. Her voice stayed calm. "But we are not planning on being late."

Marcus nodded and kept eating.

Elliot felt something shift inside him. Don't panic. Not

anger. Something quieter. A recognition that Marcus was being trained for uncertainty in the way schools trained kids for fire drills. Calm voices. Clear procedures. No one called it what it was.

After Marcus left, Kiana picked up her keys.

"I switched again today," she said. "Pickup is covered."

Elliot nodded.

"I'll call the Shelter again," he said.

Kiana held his gaze.

"Call until someone answers," she said. "Do not accept a voicemail as an answer."

Elliot nodded again, but his stomach had already hurt.

When Kiana left, the house settled into silence. Elliot sat at the table with his phone in front of him and made the call.

It rang five times.

A recording answered.

He hung up and tried again.

The second call rang longer. Then a different recording.

He tried a third time. A fourth.

On the fifth call, someone finally answered.

"Shelter case management," a woman said. Her voice was clipped, efficient.

"This is Elliot Harris," he said. "My placement was paused. I need to know what happens now."

A pause. The sound of typing.

"Yes," she said. "I see your file."

File. Always the file.

"When can I return?" Elliot asked.

"We are still under review," she replied.

"How long?" he asked.

Another pause. More typing.

"It depends," she said.

"On what?" Elliot asked, keeping his voice even.

"On compliance," she replied, as if the word answered itself. "On documentation. On availability."

Availability again. The most dishonest word in the language.

"I came to the review," Elliot said. "I signed what they asked. I did what I was told."

"Yes," the woman replied. "And that is noted."

Noted. Not solved.

"So, when can I come back?" Elliot asked.

"We can schedule a follow up appointment," she said.

"When?" he asked quickly.

"Tomorrow at eleven," she replied. "In person."

Elliot's shoulders tightened.

"I have work," he said.

"Attendance is required," she replied, the same tone Ms. Delgado used, the same tone Denise used, the same tone the nurse practitioner used. Calm. Final.

Elliot closed his eyes.

"I'll be there," he said.

"Arrive ten minutes early," she added.

Early again.

After the call, Elliot stared at the phone. The screen reflected his face. Calm. Normal. Unremarkable.

He opened his email.

There was a message from HR.

Subject line: Status Reminder

He did not open it right away. He sat for a moment, hands flat on the table, feeling the ache pulse through his wrists.

Then he opened it.

The email was short.

We have noticed continued inconsistencies. Please confirm your availability for a progress review this week.

Availability.

He closed the email and stared at the wall. His life had

become a series of rooms where people asked him to confirm what he could not control.

By midday, his body was failing in small ways. His knees burned when he stood to heat leftovers. His wrists cramped when he tried to type. He rested his forearms on the table and waited until the cramp softened.

He thought about how tired he was, and how tiredness was starting to look like his personality.

When Kiana came home in the afternoon, she walked into the kitchen and stopped when she saw him still sitting at the table.

"You get through?" she asked.

"Yes," Elliot said. "Appointment tomorrow. Eleven."

Kiana's mouth tightened.

"That is right in the middle of everything," she said.

Elliot nodded.

"They want it that way," he said, surprising himself with how certain it sounded.

Kiana stared at him.

"You said that like you know it," she said.

Elliot looked down at his hands.

"I think I do," he said.

Marcus came home with his backpack heavy and his voice loud, the way kids got when they had been holding themselves together all day.

"They asked me again," Marcus said, throwing his bag onto the floor.

Kiana looked up.

"Asked you what?" she said.

Marcus shrugged.

"Where you live," he said, looking at Elliot. "I told them I live with Mom. But then they asked where you live."

Elliot felt his stomach drop.

"What did you say?" he asked.

Marcus looked uncomfortable, like he had failed a test without knowing the rules.

"I said you used to be at the Shelter," he said. "But now you are with us. I said it was temporary."

Temporary. The word again, now in Marcus's mouth.

Elliot closed his eyes for a moment. Not long. Just long enough to feel the weight of what had been handed to his son.

"It's okay," Elliot said, forcing his voice steady. "You did not do anything wrong."

Marcus nodded, but his eyes stayed on Elliot's face.

"Ms. Delgado said she just wants to make sure everything is stable," he said.

Stable. Another word he should not have had to carry.

Kiana's expression sharpened.

"They are asking him questions like he is the messenger," she said quietly.

Elliot nodded.

"Because he is," he replied.

The room went quiet.

Marcus looked between them.

"Am I not supposed to say stuff?" he asked.

Elliot crouched slowly, his knees flaring, and tried not to show it. He rested a hand on Marcus's shoulder.

"You can always tell the truth, "He said.

Marcus held his gaze.

"Even if it gets you in trouble?" Marcus asked.

Elliot hesitated.

The honest answer rose in him and stayed there.

He swallowed.

"Yes," he said finally. "Even then."

Marcus nodded slowly, taking it in, filing it away with all the other rules he was learning.

That night, after Marcus went to bed, Elliot stood in the doorway of the small room Marcus slept in and watched him for a moment. Marcus's face was relaxed in sleep. His hands were open. He looked younger when he was not listening for adult decisions.

Elliot stepped back quietly and returned to the couch.

He opened his phone and looked at the calendar.

Tomorrow: Shelter appointment at eleven.

Work review sometime this week.

School forms pending.

City tickets due.

Nothing dramatic.

Just compression.

He lay back and stared at the ceiling. The house made small settling noises around him. Kiana moved quietly in the kitchen, cleaning again, wiping surfaces that were already clean.

Elliot understood something he had been avoiding.

He was becoming easier to manage.

Not because he was doing better.

Because he was shrinking.

11

———

Elliot arrived at The Shelter at ten forty-eight.

Early was safer.

He had left Kiana's place with enough time to account for the bus running late, for his knees locking halfway to the stop, for the kind of small delays that did not count as emergencies until you stacked them together. He moved carefully through the morning, conserving effort the way other people conserved money.

The strip mall looked the same as it had the first time. The nail salon with paper still taped to the windows. The dollar store with carts chained together like they might run. The dry cleaner with hours written in marker that could change at any moment.

From the parking lot, The Shelter still looked like a medical office that had stopped insisting it was temporary.

Inside, the lobby smelled of disinfectant and old coffee again. The television in the corner still played with the sound off. Captions scrolled. Headlines looped. Everything else stayed quiet.

Elliot checked in at the desk.

The woman who greeted him was not the same one from the intake. This woman did not smile.

"Name?" she asked.

"Elliot Harris."

She typed. Her eyes moved across the screen, then paused.

"You're here to follow up?" she asked.

"Yes," Elliot said.

She nodded without looking up.

"Take a seat," she said. "Someone will call you."

Elliot sat against the wall in a molded plastic chair and folded his hands in his lap. His wrists ached. His knees pulsed. He stared at the floor tiles, each one slightly different shade of beige, as if they had been replaced over time without anyone caring about consistency.

Men sat around him, quiet, waiting. Some held folders. Some stared at their phones. One man kept rubbing his forehead like he was trying to smooth a thought flat.

Elliot checked the time.

Ten fifty-six.

He did not want to look nervous. Nervousness looked like instability. Instability invited questions. Questions turned into notes.

At eleven twelve, a door opened and a woman stepped into the lobby holding a clipboard.

"Elliot Harris," she called.

Elliot stood slowly, his knees resisting before giving in. He followed her down a hallway that smelled cleaner than the lobby. The woman walked at a steady pace, not rushing, not slowing. Elliot adjusted his steps to match her.

She led him into an office with neutral walls and a desk that held nothing personal. No framed photos. No plants. A computer monitor. A stack of papers aligned neatly. A small sign on the desk that read "*We Are Here To Support You.*

The woman sat and motioned for him to sit.

"I'm Carla," she said. "I oversee case management reviews."

Elliot nodded.

Carla clicked her mouse and stared at the screen.

"I'm going to walk through your status," she said.

Status.

The word felt medical. The kind of word that described a condition without implying anyone could change it.

Carla spoke calmly, reading from the file like she was summarizing weather.

"You were marked absent from a required workshop," she said. "You missed check in. You left the facility during a scheduled activity window. There was an external inquiry from a school. You were placed on a temporary pause pending review."

Elliot listened without interrupting.

"I picked up my son," he said when she paused.

Carla looked at him briefly.

"We understand parenting responsibilities," she said, and Elliot felt the word understand land without weight. "But program participation is structured. When participation becomes inconsistent, we evaluate viability."

Viability.

Elliot tightened his hands in his lap until his fingers steadied.

"I'm trying to do what you ask," he said. "I came to the review. I signed. I responded to messages."

Carla nodded like she heard it often.

"Yes," she said. "And that is noted."

Noted again.

Elliot stared at the desk sign.

Support.

He waited for her to say what he needed her to say.

Carla turned the monitor slightly, not enough for him to read it fully, just enough for him to see there was a list.

"Here's the outcome," she said. "Your pause will be extended."

Elliot felt his chest tighten.

"For how long?" he asked.

Carla's expression stayed calm.

"At this time, we cannot provide an exact timeframe," she said. "It depends on capacity, review outcomes, and demonstrated reliability."

Elliot blinked.

"How do I demonstrate reliability if I'm not there?" he asked.

Carla paused, then answered as if it was simple.

"By remaining reachable," she said. "By attending scheduled appointments. By providing documentation when requested."

Documentation.

Elliot leaned forward slightly.

"So, I'm still in the program," he said, trying to keep his voice steady.

Carla's eyes returned to the screen.

"You will be moved to inactive status," she said. "That means you are not currently placed, but you remain eligible for reentry pending future review."

Inactive.

The word made him feel like an object.

"What does inactive mean in practical terms?" he asked.

Carla reached for a stack of papers and slid them across the desk.

"It means you will not have a bed here," she said. "It means you will need to seek alternative shelter options until placement becomes available."

Elliot stared at the papers. They were printed lists. Phone numbers. Addresses. Intake hours. Requirements in small text.

A list of places that might not have space.

A list of waiting rooms.

A list of rules.

Carla continued, voice still calm.

"If you secure stable housing elsewhere, that is positive," she said. "If you do not, we encourage you to access emergency shelters. We can also connect you with employment support resources remotely."

Employment support.

He thought of Denise's folder. The weekly review. The word availability.

He looked up.

"My job expects me there," he said. "This appointment is right in the middle of the day."

Carla nodded again.

"We understand that can be challenging," she said.

Challenging. Another soft word.

Elliot's mouth went dry.

"So, what am I supposed to do now?" he asked.

Carla's expression did not change.

"You're supposed to remain engaged," she said. "Remain reachable. Follow up. Comply with any requests. This will support future review."

Support future review.

The room stayed quiet.

Elliot looked at the papers again. He saw familiar language repeated across the list.

Eligibility. Intake. Proof. Required.

He felt his wrists begin to throb harder, as if his body had finally caught up to what was being said.

Carla held a pen out toward him.

"I need your signature acknowledging receipt of the outcome," she said.

Elliot stared at the line.

His wrist cramped as he picked up the pen. He signed anyway.

Carla took the papers back, placed them neatly in a folder, then handed the folder to him like it was a gift.

"Do you have any questions?" she asked.

Elliot almost laughed, but there was no room in his body for laughter.

"No," he said.

Carla stood.

"Thank you for coming," she said. "Stay reachable."

Elliot walked out holding the folder against his chest.

In the lobby, the television captions kept scrolling. The same men sat along the walls. A new name was called. Someone stood. Someone sat.

Nothing changed.

Outside, the cold air hit him hard. He stood by the door for a moment, folder in hand, and looked at the strip mall. People came and went from the dollar store. Cars pulled in and pulled out. The world moved without needing permission.

Elliot checked his phone.

Two missed calls from Denise.

A new email notification.

He did not open it yet.

He called her back.

She answered on the second ring.

"Elliot," she said. Her voice was calm. Always calm. "Where are you?"

"I had an appointment," he said. "I told you I needed the time."

"Yes," Denise replied. "And that is noted."

He closed his eyes.

"I'm coming in now," he said.

Denise paused.

"We need you in my office tomorrow morning," she said. "Nine thirty. Progress review."

Progress review.

Elliot's throat tightened.

"I'll be there," he said.

"Thank you," Denise replied, relief entering her voice as if agreement solved something. "Try to keep this week consistent."

Consistent.

Elliot ended the call and stared at the folder.

He did not open the list.

He already knew what it would ask.

By the time he returned to Kiana's house, his knees were shaking from the walk. His wrists burned. He moved through the door carefully, trying not to show it.

Kiana looked up from the counter immediately.

"What happened?" she asked.

Elliot held the folder out.

"They extended it," he said. "Inactive status."

Kiana's mouth tightened.

"So, you're out," she said.

"They won't say it like that," Elliot replied.

Kiana took the folder and flipped it open, scanning the pages. Her eyes moved quickly, reading the same language over and over.

"These are just lists," she said.

Elliot nodded.

"They call it resources," he said.

Kiana looked up.

"They want you to remain reachable," she said.

Elliot nodded again.

"Every place wants me reachable," he said. "None of them want me to rest."

Marcus came into the room then, backpack on, face bright from the day.

"Dad," he said, then paused when he saw the folder. "What's that?"

Elliot forced his face into something gentle.

"Just papers," he said.

Marcus stepped closer and looked at Kiana.

"Did they let you back?" Marcus asked.

Elliot hesitated.

Kiana answered, careful.

"Not yet," she said. "They're still deciding."

Marcus nodded slowly, like he had expected it.

He looked back at Elliot.

"Are you staying here again?" he asked.

Elliot swallowed.

"For now," he said.

Marcus accepted the answer the way he accepted all the other temporary answers in his life. He went to the table and pulled out his homework.

Elliot sat on the edge of the couch and stared at his hands.

Kiana stood beside him for a moment, then said quietly, "The school sent the emergency contact form again."

Elliot looked up.

"They want a backup," she continued. "Someone they can call if you don't answer."

Elliot nodded once.

"Put whoever you need," he said.

Kiana studied him.

"You're making yourself smaller," she said.

Elliot stared at the floor.

"I'm making myself easier," he replied.

The room went quiet.

Marcus's pencil scratched across paper at the table. The

sound was steady, controlled, like the only thing in the house that still made sense.

Elliot sat there with the folder beside him on the couch.

A list of places.

A list of rules.

A list that did not include him.

He did not open it again.

He already knew what it meant to be inactive.

It meant his absence had become official.

12

—————

Elliot stopped setting alarms.

Not all at once. At first, he just stopped adjusting to them. Then he stopped adding new reminders. The calendar on his phone stayed full, but he stopped believing it could protect him. He woke before it anyway, the way he always did, his body was already tense with anticipation.

Morning arrived quietly at Kiana's house, the same way it had for days now. The couch remembered him. The blanket held the shape of his shoulders. He rose carefully, testing his knees, rubbing his wrists until feeling returned.

He did not hurry.

There was nowhere he was expected to be on time anymore.

In the kitchen, Kiana was already dressed, coffee mug in hand, eyes on her phone.

"They didn't reply," she said without looking up.

Elliot nodded.

"They will," he said, though he no longer believed it meant anything.

Marcus came in a few minutes later, backpack on, shoes

tied properly this time. He had started tying them tighter. He did not ask Elliot if he was coming along.

"I'll walk myself to the corner," Marcus said. "Mom said it's okay."

Elliot nodded.

"I'll watch," he said.

Marcus shrugged, already halfway to the door.

Outside, Elliot stood by the window and watched Marcus walk down the block. He did not rush. He did not look back. He moved like someone who had learned where the edges were.

When Marcus turned the corner, Elliot stepped away from the window.

The house felt larger in the quiet that followed.

Elliot sat at the table and opened his laptop. He stared at the screen without touching the keyboard. His inbox refreshed automatically.

No new messages from the Shelter.

No updates from HR.

No requests from the school.

The absence felt deliberate.

He closed the laptop and leaned back, hands resting on his thighs. His wrists throbbed faintly. His knees ached. He waited for the familiar spike of urgency that never came.

By late morning, he walked to the corner store and bought milk and bread with money he had been careful not to spend. The clerk nodded without looking up. The receipt printed slowly. Elliot folded it and put it in his pocket like evidence of movement.

On the walk back, he passed a bus stop where a man stood reading a notice taped to the pole. Elliot recognized the look. The way the shoulders tensed. The way the mouth tightened slightly.

He kept walking.

At noon, Denise emailed.

Just checking in. Let me know your availability.

Availability again.

Elliot stared at the message.

He did not reply right away.

He made lunch. He ate slowly. He washed the plate and dried it immediately instead of leaving it in the rack. Small acts of order that did not get recorded anywhere.

When he finally replied, he kept it short.

I'm available after three.

The response came quickly.

Thank you. We'll circle back.

Circle back meant nothing would change.

In the afternoon, the school sent another form. This one asked for confirmation of emergency contacts and dismissal plans. The language was polite. Neutral. Firm.

Elliot read it twice, then forwarded it to Kiana without comment.

He did not offer suggestions.

He had learned that offering suggestions invited scrutiny.

When Marcus came home, he dropped his backpack by the door and went straight to the table.

"I gotta finish this," he said, already pulling out a worksheet.

Elliot watched him work. The careful way Marcus lined up numbers. The way he erased lightly to avoid tearing the paper.

"They didn't ask about you today," Marcus said suddenly.

Elliot looked up.

"At school," Marcus clarified. "They didn't ask where you live."

Elliot nodded.

"Okay," he said.

Marcus waited, then added, "Ms. Delgado just said to make sure my homework gets done."

Elliot felt something loosen in his chest that he did not fully trust.

"That's good," he said.

Marcus shrugged and kept writing.

That night, after Marcus went to bed, Elliot sat alone on the couch. The folder from the Shelter still sat beside him, unopened. He had stopped moving it from place to place. It had become part of the room.

He opened his phone and scrolled through old messages. Missed calls. Reminders. Requests that no longer came.

He realized that no one had asked him to explain himself all day.

The relief surprised him.

So did the cost.

He thought about how easy it had become to stay quiet. How natural it felt to stay out of the way. How his body seemed to welcome the reduction in demand even as something else in him resisted it.

Elliot understood then that the system did not need him to disappear.

It just needed him to stop insisting on being counted.

Outside, a bus passed, brakes hissing, then moving on. Elliot watched the reflection slide across the wall and fade.

He did not follow it.

He stayed where he was, quiet, compliant, present in a way that did not register.

And the house held him like it always had.

Not because he belonged.

But because there was nowhere else asking for him.

13

———

On Monday, Elliot received a call from a number he did not recognize.

He watched it ring once, then twice, then stopped. He stared at the screen as if it might explain itself. For a moment, his body prepared for urgency the way it used to. Chest tightening. Shoulders rising. Hands bracing against the old expectation that something was about to be demanded.

Then the feeling passed.

The phone buzzed again.

A voicemail notification.

He did not listen to it right away.

He made coffee instead. He stood at the counter and watched the dark liquid fill the mug, steady and obedient. He drank it slowly, letting the warmth do what it could. His wrists ached faintly. His knees held their usual complaint, but the pain felt quieter these days, less insulted. His body had stopped expecting kindness from time.

Kiana had already left for work. Marcus had already left for school. The house was empty in the way it had become empty. Not lonely. Just unclaimed.

Elliot sat at the table and opened his laptop.

No new emails from the Shelter.

No new emails from HR.

No new forms from the school.

The absence was held.

He clicked the voicemail.

A woman's voice filled the room, calm and professional.

"Mr. Harris, this is Mrs. Landon from Marcus's school. Please give me a call back at your earliest convenience. We would like to schedule a brief meeting to discuss Marcus's support plan and ensure we are aligned moving forward. Thank you."

Aligned again.

Elliot stared at the screen.

A brief meeting was never brief. A support plan was never just support. Aligned means documented. It meant decisions made politely. It meant being asked to confirm what had already been written down.

He closed the laptop and sat still.

He thought about calling back. He thought about showing up. He thought about how he used to walk into school buildings like he belonged there, not as a father on review, but as a professional. A man with keys and an ID badge. A man with a classroom. A man whose name was said without hesitation.

He thought about how long it had been since anyone had asked what he thought was best for Marcus.

His phone buzzed again.

A text.

Kiana.

School called you?

Elliot typed back.

Yes.

A pause.

Another message.

They called me too. Meeting request.

Elliot stared at the phone.

He could feel the impulse to respond correctly. To choose the safest words. To keep things smooth. Smooth was survival now.

He typed.

Do what you think is best.

He sent it before he could edit it.

A few minutes later, another message arrived.

I want you there.

Elliot held the phone in both hands.

He did not answer right away.

He stood up and walked to the window. Outside, the street looked ordinary. A bus rolling past. A man walking a dog. A woman dragging a trash bin back up her driveway. Nothing in the air suggested a decision was waiting.

Elliot rested his forehead against the glass.

He could go.

He could sit in that room again, in a chair meant for compliance. He could explain himself. He could choose the right tone, careful and grateful. He could offer a plan. He could show proof. He could try to be legible.

He could also watch the way their eyes moved. The way the folder opened. The way words like support and stability arrived before the request for documentation.

He could sit there and feel his body ache and keep his face calm.

He could go and become part of the record again.

His knees throbbed as he stood, reminding him what movement cost now.

He walked back to the table and typed.

I don't think it helps for me to be there.

He stared at the message.

It sounded smaller than he felt. It sounded like surrender even though it was not meant to be. It sounded like the kind of sentence people used when they were trying to make someone else comfortable.

He deleted it.

He typed again.

I can't make it.

He deleted that too.

He typed a third time.

I'm not in a place to sit in that room right now.

He sent it.

The message left his phone and became final.

He waited for the response.

Kiana replied a few minutes later.

Okay.

Just that.

No argument. No guilt. No reassurance.

Elliot read the word again. The single syllable sat in his chest like a closed door.

He put the phone down and sat at the table, hands resting flat. His wrists pulsed faintly. His fingers looked normal. His hands did not.

For the first time in a long time, Elliot noticed how quiet his own mind had become. Not peaceful. Just quiet. The part of him that used to rehearse speeches and anticipate questions had gone still, like it had learned that preparation did not change outcomes.

Later that afternoon, Denise emailed.

Checking in. We have an opening for your progress review tomorrow at 9:30.

Elliot stared at the message.

Progress review. Another room. Another folder.

He wrote back.

I can't do it tomorrow morning. Afternoon only.

He hesitated, then added a second sentence.

I will be present when required.

He read it twice before sending it.

Present when required.

Not present because it mattered. Not present because he had something to contribute. Present because absence would be punished.

He sent it anyway.

At three thirty, Marcus came home quieter than usual.

He dropped his backpack by the door and went straight to the table. He sat without being told and pulled out his homework.

Kiana walked in behind him, face unreadable, holding a sheet of paper.

Elliot looked up.

"How was school?" he asked Marcus.

Marcus shrugged.

Kiana set the paper on the counter and did not speak right away. She took her coat off slowly, like she needed time to choose the right words.

"They want a formal plan," she said finally.

Elliot nodded.

"What kind of plan?" he asked, though he already knew.

"A support plan," Kiana replied. "For Marcus. Attendance. Dismissal. Home stability. They want it all in writing."

Elliot felt his throat tighten.

"And what did you say?" he asked.

Kiana looked at him.

"I said we are doing our best," she replied. "I said you have health issues. I said the housing situation is temporary."

Temporary again.

Elliot nodded as if agreement could protect them.

Marcus looked up from his worksheet.

"Am I in trouble?" he asked.

Elliot stood slowly, his knees protesting, and walked to the table. He crouched beside Marcus, careful, keeping his face calm.

"No," Elliot said. "You're not in trouble."

Marcus studied him.

"Then why do they keep making plans about me?" he asked.

Elliot opened his mouth.

The truth rose up, clear and sharp, but it did not fit in a child's room. Not cleanly. Not safely.

Kiana stepped closer and placed a hand on the back of Marcus's chair.

"They want to help," she said, her voice gentle.

Marcus nodded, accepting the sentence without believing it fully. He went back to his homework.

Elliot stayed crouched for a moment longer than necessary. His knees burned. His wrists throbbed. He felt the weight of what he had not said settle inside him.

He stood and moved back to the couch, lowering himself carefully.

Kiana watched him.

"You should've come," she said quietly. Not accusing. Not angry. Just the truth.

Elliot nodded.

"I know," he replied.

Kiana sat across from him, elbows on her knees.

"They talked like you weren't here anyway," she said. "Like you were an idea. Like you were a variable."

Elliot stared at his hands.

"That's what I am now," he said.

Kiana's eyes sharpened.

"You're Marcus's father," she said.

Elliot nodded again, but he did not lift his head.

"I know," he said.

The room went quiet.

Marcus's pencil scratched steadily across paper at the table, the sound consistent, controlled, like the only thing in the house that still moved in straight lines.

Elliot sat on the couch and felt something settle in him with calm certainty.

There had been a time when he believed showing up would protect him.

Now he understood that showing up was not protection.

Showing up was participation.

He did not know what it meant to refuse participation without losing everything.

He only knew he had started refusing in small ways. A missed call. A declined room. A sentence left unsaid.

Not rebellion. Not drama.

Just quiet withdrawal.

And once he noticed it, he realized something else.

He did not miss the rooms.

He missed the version of himself that used to walk into them.

14

———

The letter arrived on a Thursday.

It was folded once and slipped between grocery flyers and a credit card offer, the kind of envelope that didn't announce itself as important. Elliot almost missed it. He stood at the counter sorting mail into piles that no longer meant much. Bills he already knew were coming. Notices that could wait. Things addressed to Kiana. Things addressed to Marcus.

This one had his name on it.

He recognized the school's return address immediately.

He did not open it right away.

He set it on the counter and made lunch instead. Soup from a can. He heated it slowly, stirring even when it didn't need stirring. His wrists complained. His knees held steady. The small mercies arrived without pattern now.

He ate standing up.

The envelope stayed where it was.

After lunch, he sat at the table and opened it carefully, like the paper might react to haste.

The letter was brief. Polite. Precise.

Dear Mr. Harris,

We are writing to inform you of an update to Marcus's student support plan. Effective immediately, all primary school communication will be directed to Ms. Thompson to ensure consistency and timely response. You will continue to be listed as an emergency contact.

Thank you for your cooperation.

Cooperation.

Elliot read it twice.

Primary school communication.

Emergency contact.

The words rearranged his position without asking his permission. He was still there, technically. Listed. Reachable. But no longer central. No longer expected to respond. No longer someone whose availability required negotiation.

He folded the letter back along the crease and placed it in the folder with the others. The folder had grown thick without him noticing.

He did not feel angry.

The absence of anger surprised him.

Later that afternoon, Denise emailed.

We've adjusted your workload temporarily to reduce strain. Please focus on core tasks only. We'll revisit expectations next quarter.

Reduce strain.

Core tasks.

Temporary again.

Elliot read the message, then closed his laptop without replying. The adjustment felt like relief and erasure at the same time.

At three thirty, Marcus came home carrying his backpack differently. Higher on his shoulders. More secure.

"Mom says I can walk home with Ben now," Marcus said, dropping his bag by the door.

Elliot looked up. "From school?"

"Yeah," Marcus said. "Ben's mom walks with us until the corner."

Elliot nodded.

"Okay," he said.

Marcus hesitated.

"They said it's fine," he added quickly. "They just need Mom to sign the form."

Elliot nodded again.

"That makes sense," he said.

Marcus studied his face for a moment, as if checking whether this was something that required discussion. Then he shrugged and went to the table to start his homework.

Elliot sat back on the couch and felt the quiet settle.

That evening, Kiana handed him another form.

"This just needs my signature," she said. "It's about dismissal. Walking permission."

Elliot glanced at it.

"Do you want me to sign too?" he asked.

Kiana paused.

"They didn't ask for it," she said.

Elliot nodded.

"Okay," he replied.

She signed and set the paper aside.

Neither of them mentioned the letter.

After Marcus went to bed, Elliot sat alone in the living room. The folder rested on the coffee table now, open, its contents spread slightly like they wanted air.

School letters. Shelter lists. HR notices. Forms with check-boxes and careful language.

A record of adjustment.

He realized then that no one had formally removed him from anything.

They had simply rerouted around him.

The next morning, Elliot walked Marcus to the corner

without being asked. Marcus waited with Ben and Ben's mother, chatting easily. When it was time, Marcus waved once and turned away.

Elliot stood there a moment longer than necessary, then walked home alone.

At the house, he sat at the table and stared at the empty chair across from him. He thought about how many times he had been told consistency mattered. How often he had been measured against it.

He understood now that consistency was not about presence.

It was about predictability.

And unpredictability, once named, was managed by removal.

That afternoon, his phone rang.

It was the Shelter.

He let it ring.

The voicemail arrived. Calm. Professional. Asking him to confirm availability for a future review.

He deleted it.

Not because he was angry.

Because it no longer felt addressed to him.

That night, as he lay on the couch, knees aching softly, wrists warm under the blanket, Elliot thought about the rooms he no longer entered.

School offices. Shelter offices. Conference rooms with neutral walls.

He had imagined absence would feel like loss.

Instead, it felt like being edited out mid-sentence.

The story continued.

It just no longer paused for him.

15

———————

On Saturday morning, Elliot walked to the park.

Not because anyone suggested it. Not because it was on a plan. Not because it was part of a routine he was trying to rebuild. He walked because the day was clear and quiet and he needed to be somewhere that did not require proof.

The park was four blocks away; a small rectangle of grass and trees squeezed between row homes and a busy street. The swings creaked. The basketball court had one bent rim. A few parents sat on benches watching children climb and fall and climb again.

Elliot moved slowly, letting his knees set the pace. His wrists ached faintly, but the cold air loosened the stiffness enough to make walking possible. He kept his hands in his pockets and looked straight ahead.

Marcus was not with him.

That was the first thought that landed.

On Saturdays, Marcus used to come with him. They would throw a ball back and forth, small and uneven throws that Marcus laughed at when Elliot pretended to miss. They would sit on the bench with pretzels from the corner store and watch the older kids ride bikes too fast.

Now Marcus spent Saturdays with Kiana's sister, or at Ben's house, or at birthday parties Elliot learned about after they happened.

No one had told Elliot he could not come.

The invitations simply stopped arriving.

Elliot sat on a bench near the playground and watched a boy climb the ladder to the slide. The boy hesitated at the top, looked back at his mother, then went down anyway.

Elliot thought about how children learned what to expect by watching how adults responded. How quickly they adjusted to whatever stayed consistent.

He checked his phone.

One missed call.

Unknown number.

He did not call back.

A text from Kiana came through.

Marcus wants to know if you can come by later. He has a project due.

Elliot stared at the message.

He felt an old instinct to answer immediately. To prove responsiveness. To show reliability. He could almost hear Mrs. Landon's voice in his head. Timely response. Consistency. Alignment.

He breathed in slowly and let the air settle.

He typed back.

Yes. What time?

A reply came quickly.

Around 3.

Elliot nodded to himself, as if the decision had been made by someone else.

He sat on the bench and watched the park move. Two teenagers arguing quietly near the court. A man jogging with headphones in. A little girl pulled her coat sleeves over her hands.

Nobody here asked him for documentation.

Nobody here asked him to confirm anything.

The quiet felt like relief and like grief at the same time.

At three, Elliot walked to Kiana's place.

He arrived early.

Early was safer.

Kiana opened the door and stepped aside. She looked tired but not surprised to see him. Tired was the new normal in her face too.

Marcus was at the table with a poster board spread out in front of him. Markers. Glue sticks. Printed pictures. A worksheet with instructions in a small font.

"Dad," Marcus said, looking up.

Elliot smiled. "Hey."

Marcus held up the worksheet.

"It's about families," he said. "We gotta make a family tree."

Elliot's stomach tightened slightly.

"Okay," he said. "Show me what you need."

Marcus pointed to the paper. "We gotta list people we live with and people who help us. Then we gotta put their jobs in."

Their jobs.

Elliot sat beside him, moving carefully into the chair. His knees complained, then settled. He leaned over the worksheet and read the prompts.

Who lives in your home?

Who picks you up from school?

Who helps you with homework?

Who is your emergency contact?

Elliot felt his wrists ache as he picked up a marker.

Kiana stood at the counter pretending to do something with dishes that were already clean.

Marcus started writing without hesitation.

Mom.

Aunt Tasha.

Ben's mom sometimes.

Grandma on FaceTime.

Elliot watched the words appear.

Marcus added another line.

Dad.

Then he paused, marker hovering.

"Do I write where you live?" Marcus asked quietly.

Elliot's throat tightened.

Kiana stopped moving.

"It doesn't ask that," Elliot said gently.

Marcus looked down at the paper.

"But Ms. Delgado said we gotta be accurate," Marcus said. "She said it matters."

Elliot rested his hand on the table.

"You can be accurate without giving them everything," he said.

Marcus frowned slightly, trying to understand.

"Is that lying?" he asked.

Elliot shook his head.

"No," he said. "It's choosing what belongs to you."

Marcus stared at him, the way he did when he was trying to file a new rule.

Kiana walked over and sat across from them.

"They shouldn't be giving kids assignments like this," she said quietly. Her voice was controlled, but there was heat under it.

Elliot nodded.

"They call it engagement," he said.

Marcus looked between them.

"So what do I put?" he asked.

Elliot leaned closer to the worksheet.

"Put what's true," he said. "You live with Mom. Dad helps you. Dad is your dad."

Marcus nodded slowly and wrote.

Dad helps me.

Then he looked up.

"Do you pick me up?" Marcus asked, not accusing, just checking.

Elliot felt the question land in him like a weight.

"Not right now," he said softly.

Marcus nodded, accepting it.

"But you want to," Marcus said, as if offering him a way back in.

Elliot swallowed.

"Yes," he said. "I want to."

Marcus went back to writing.

When the project was finished, Marcus held it up proudly.

Elliot smiled. "You did good."

Marcus beamed, then looked toward Kiana.

"Can I show Ms. Delgado Monday?" he asked.

Kiana nodded.

Elliot watched Marcus run to his room to put it in his backpack.

When Marcus was gone, Kiana looked at Elliot.

"He asks me questions now," she said quietly. "About you. About where you are. About why things change."

Elliot nodded.

"I know," he said.

Kiana held his gaze.

"You don't have to disappear," she said.

Elliot stared at his hands.

"I didn't leave," he said.

Kiana exhaled, slow.

"You got rerouted," she said.

Elliot nodded, almost a smile.

"Yeah," he said. "I got rerouted."

They sat in silence for a moment.

From Marcus's room, they could hear him humming softly as he organized his backpack.

Elliot felt something shift in him then.

Not hope.

Clarity.

He understood now that fatherhood was not something the systems could give him or take from him. But they could make it smaller. They could make it conditional. They could make it something he had to perform in ways that could be documented.

He looked up at Kiana.

"I don't know how to fight them," he said. "Not without losing what little I still get to have."

Kiana nodded once.

"I know," she said.

Elliot listened to Marcus humming in the next room and felt the truth settle fully.

He was still Marcus's father.

But the world had trained Marcus to ask for him differently.

And once a child learned how to adjust, the adjustment did not feel like a loss.

It felt like life.

On Sunday evening, Elliot walked Marcus back to Kiana's place after dinner.

The sky was already dim, the light thinning into that gray that made everything look unfinished. Streetlights flickered on one by one, not dramatic, just necessary. Cars passed without slowing. Somewhere down the block, someone laughed loudly and then stopped.

Marcus walked a half step ahead of him, swinging his backpack even though there was nothing inside it.

"Are you coming to my thing this week?" Marcus asked.

Elliot knew which thing he meant without asking.

"The presentation?" Elliot said.

Marcus nodded. "We gotta stand in front of the class and talk about our family tree."

Elliot felt the question arrive before Marcus finished speaking.

"What day?" he asked.

"Wednesday," Marcus said. "After lunch."

Elliot did the math automatically. The time. The walk. The

meetings that might appear without warning. The rooms he no longer entered.

"I'll try," he said.

Marcus didn't nod right away this time.

"Mom's coming," he said. "She already said yes."

Elliot nodded.

"That's good," he said.

They reached the corner and stopped. Kiana was waiting by the door, arms crossed loosely, watching them approach.

Marcus turned and hugged Elliot quickly, the way older kids did when they didn't want to linger.

"See you," Marcus said.

Elliot smiled. "See you."

Marcus went inside without looking back.

Elliot stood on the sidewalk for a moment longer than necessary. He watched the door close. He watched the light inside shift as people moved.

Then he turned and walked home alone.

At Kiana's place later, Elliot sat on the couch while Kiana filled out another form at the table.

"They added a new section," she said without looking up. "Just checkboxes. Who attends school events. Who handles communication."

Elliot nodded.

"Put whatever keeps it smooth," he said.

Kiana paused and looked at him.

"They don't mean to erase you," she said.

Elliot nodded again.

"I know," he said. "They just don't need me to be visible."

Kiana went back to the form.

That night, Elliot lay awake on the couch, listening to the house settle. His knees ached softly. His wrists rested heavily against his chest. The pain was familiar now, a low constant that no longer startled him.

He thought about Wednesday.

He imagined Marcus standing at the front of the room holding his poster board. He imagined Kiana sitting in a small chair, smiling encouragement. He imagined Ms. Delgado nodding politely.

He imagined the space where he would not be sitting.

Not empty.

Just unnecessary.

In the morning, Elliot woke up early and made coffee. He drank it standing at the counter, watching light creep across the floor. His phone buzzed once.

A reminder.

Shelter follow up pending.

He cleared it without opening it.

Later, he walked to the park again. He sat on the same bench as before. The swings creaked. A boy fell and got back up without crying. A woman called out encouragement from her phone.

Elliot sat with his hands in his pockets and watched.

No one asked him why he was there.

No one asked him to explain himself.

He thought about how often he had been told that showing up mattered.

He thought about how quietly that rule had changed.

By the time he stood to leave, the light had shifted again. The park emptied slowly, not all at once. People left when they were ready.

Elliot walked home at his own pace.

At the door, he paused and rested his hand against the frame, feeling the solidness of it. Something that stayed.

Inside, the house was quiet.

Elliot sat on the couch and looked around the room. The folder lay on the table, still unopened. The forms were stacked neatly beside it.

He did not reach for them.

Instead, he picked up a pen and a blank piece of paper from the counter. He wrote Marcus's name at the top.

Below it, he wrote his own.

He looked at the two names for a long time.

Then he folded the paper once and slipped it into his pocket.

Outside, a bus passed, brakes hissing softly, then pulling away.

Elliot stayed where he was.

He was still there.

And that was the part no one was counting anymore.

ABOUT THE AUTHOR

Khaled Ashraf is a writer and school leader whose work examines fatherhood and the institutional systems that quietly define worth. Grounded in lived experience across education and public service, his writing explores the politics of visibility, accountability, and belonging. The Shelter is his debut novel.